MANIFOLD SINS

A Novel

by

Margaret Boland

Manifold Sins
This is a work of fiction and all characters are created from the imagination of the writer. Any resemblance to persons living or dead is purely coincidental.

FIRST EDITION
First Printing 2008

ISBN: 0-9759397-4-2
978-0-9759397-4-1

Cover and art design by Carolyn Mayson Miller Design

Printed in the United States

Magnolia Mansions Press
Mobile, Alabama

IN LOVING MEMORY OF MY
BELOVED DAUGHTER

Peg of my Heart

"Almighty God, Father of our Lord Jesus Christ, Maker of all things, Judge of all men; we acknowledge and bewail our manifold sins and wickedness, which we, from time to time, most grievously have committed, by thought, word and deed against thy Divine Majesty, provoking most justly thy wrath and indignation against us......."

The Book of Common Prayer, 1928

CHAPTER ONE

Lee Castleberry

It was raining the first time I saw the school. The gray overcast day reflected my mood. I hated the sight of the building. I never aspired to be a school teacher, and heaven knows I avoided Mickey Mouse 101 courses with a vengeance. But now I needed a job. Any job at this point.

And William Robert Slaughter, whom we always called Billy Bob in college days, had offered me a position.

"Come do our public relations," he said. "With all your newspaper background, you're a natural. We can't pay a whole lot, but anything is better than nothing, right?"

Yeah, right. I must be out of my mind to take him up on it, but my wallet was empty, the cupboard was bare, and the fridge out of beer. I needed funds quickly to go to the grocery store.

I looked up at the large live oak tree that grew beside the drive leading to the front of the building. Its long branches spread out over the pavement making a canopy of sorts. I'd learn later it was called "Old Annie". And Old Annie was to fall in a storm in the future. So was I, but I didn't know it at this time–and neither did Old Annie. We both just stood there with a fine misty rain surrounding and drifting down on us.

I took a deep breath and headed toward the door. I pushed it open and entered a hall that looked as if it hadn't been swept in the last ten years. It hadn't. The building had just been purchased by St. Bonaventure Church to house its independent school system which went kindergarten through high school. I'd found out there were about one thousand students, boys and girls, who attended this institution and they had outgrown the "little school in the church basement".

I looked around and saw that a great deal of work would be needed to get the place ready for the students who were scheduled to arrive in the next two weeks.

I walked on down the corridor but saw no one. I peeped into a room off the hall. All I saw was some chairs and a table, a few books on the shelves that lined the walls and more dust.

What the hell have I got myself into? I thought. I stepped back out into the hall and bumped right into Billy Bob Slaughter.

"Lee," he smiled. "There you are. We've been waiting for you. Man, I can't tell you how glad I am that you've come on board with St. Bonaventure. Come on upstairs and meet the rest of the team."

I followed him up some stairs and into a large room which had a beautiful rectangular mahogany table in the center, and around which four or five people were already seated.

Billy Bob introduced me; we both took chairs with the group at the table.

"We've got a lot of work to do," Billy Bob began. "School opens in exactly eighteen days. We'll all have to pitch in and work night and day to be ready. But, I think we have the team that can do this thing. We're going to make Saint Bonnie the best independent school in the state before we're done. So let's get started."

I tried to listen and stay alert as Billy Bob droned on and on about the need for structural repairs, supplies to be ordered, interviews with a few more new teachers, assignment of students, readying the classrooms, setting up the lunchroom. The more he talked the more I wished I was still unemployed. As yet I had no idea what my part in this grand scheme was going to be, and I wasn't sure I wanted to know.

I found out soon enough. "Lee," said Billy Bob, "We're counting on you to organize our first football team. We don't have many senior boys this year, but you can get a Junior Varsity team going and play a few games. We have to start somewhere."

That got my attention. If I'd had any sense, I'd have protested right then and there, but I was too embarrassed to say before the whole group that Billy Bob had hired me to do public relations, and that I knew absolutely nothing about coaching, let alone coaching football, that I had no teaching certificate, and that I wished with all my heart that I were somewhere else.

But I hadn't had lunch and my growing hunger kept me quiet. I suppose I could read some how-to-coach books, I thought. Anyway, I couldn't bring myself to get into any confrontation at that time.

I studied the group around the table. Malcolm Grubbs was

the designated upper school director, whatever that meant. He was slightly balding, a little on the pudgy side and wore horn rimmed glasses. Sally Struthers was to be head of the middle and elementary school. She, too, was on the heavy side. Did all educators tend to be over weight? Was that to be my fate in a few years? No, I didn't intend to stay that long. One school year and I'd be out of here.

Next at the table was Grace Garland, introduced as the head of the curriculum. That didn't mean anything to me either, but she was a very attractive woman who looked to be about my own age. I checked her hands to see if there was the ring on the third finger left hand, but she kept her hands in her lap most of the time and it was hard for me to determine if she even wore a ring. She had beautiful brown eyes, chestnut brown hair and olive complexion. Looking at Grace Garland was the only really enjoyable thing I'd found so far in the day. When she spoke of the required subjects we would be offering at St. Bonaventure, her voice was low and husky. She made me want to sign up for Advanced English and Literature there on the spot if she would teach the class.

We finally adjourned and to my way of thinking, I couldn't see much of anything had been accomplished. Billy Bob got called to some duty as the meeting broke up, and I wandered the halls again. This time it was my good fortune to find Grace Garland coming out of a classroom as I passed.

"Hello again, Lee," she said and smiled broadly. "I was just going to the cafeteria to see if the Cokes had come in yet. Won't you join me in a refreshing drink?"

"You're going to let the students have Cokes?" I found that hard to believe.

"No, they'll get milk. The Cokes will go to the faculty lounge in time. But for now, we should be able to get one in the cafeteria if they've been delivered."

We walked down the hall and turned and entered a large room which was obviously the cafeteria. I was feeling better about being here—at least if I forgot that I was supposed to coach football. If only I could just talk and drink Cokes with Grace Garland all day, maybe life at St. Bonnie would be tolerable.

We were able to get our cold drinks and we moved to a table and sat down.

"Where did you coach last year?" Grace asked.

"I-er-well, I didn't coach anywhere," I stammered. "Billy Bob and I go back to frat house days at the University, and he prevailed on me to come help him get St. Bonnie, I mean St. Bonaventure, set up and running in this new building. He said I would be doing public relations. That's my field. I didn't know a thing about the football coaching until Billy Bob threw that assignment at me at the meeting."

Grace studied me and took a sip of her Coke. "I see," she said. "And do you have any background in education at all?"

"I'm afraid not. Do you think I should stay or go?"

"Oh stay by all means. I didn't mean that to have a negative connotation. In fact in spite of being in charge of the curriculum, I don't put too much stock in the schools of education that stress a lot of educational philosophy and don't bother to have teachers learn the subject they teach."

I felt a little better when Grace Garland said that. I wondered if she knew any football plays.

Billy Bob entered the cafeteria at that moment. "Oh, there you are," he said. "Come with me and I'll show you your office in the gym."

With regret I said goodbye to Grace Garland and followed Billy Bob out of the cafeteria to an adjoining building which was the gym. He led me to a little cubby hole under the grandstand and into a wire cage where there were floor to ceiling shelves filled with football helmets, pants, shirts, and racks of footballs and basketballs. Beyond the storage room was a small office with a single desk and chair.

"It's all yours," Billy Bob beamed.

"Billy Bob, I didn't want to bring this up in front of the committee or whatever you call the group we met with. I didn't want to embarrass you or me in front of those other people, but you know I know nothing about coaching football."

"No problem, you'll learn," Billy Bob said. "Just get something started and we can get a real coach next year."

"Next year! Thanks a lot. That sounds like an exciting and promising future."

"Don't be so touchy, Lee. I need you to help me build this place, and I know you can do anything when you put your mind to it." Billy Bob smiled again.

He turned to leave. "I'll let you get settled in your new office. You'll need to inventory the equipment and order what you need to outfit the team. We'll have a telephone in your office by tomorrow so you can get started on the football schedule."

And he left me there amid the helmets and the deflated footballs. I took a deep breath and then wished I hadn't as the area smelled like the locker room I guess it was.

I really think if it hadn't been for Grace Garland, I would have turned and walked away from the whole thing right then and there. Maybe it would have been better if I had. But I didn't and what a difference it has made in my life.

Grace Garland

So this is the boy wonder I thought when Billy Bob Slaughter came into the meeting room with the new staff member, Lee Castleberry. We all wondered what he'd be like after Billy Bob announced that his old college chum was coming to make a difference in the beginning of the new St. Bonaventure. We have this big new building that was bought from the Sacred Heart Brothers. It was a three storied brick structure in good repair and had been used as a Scholastic Training School for the order. But the numbers had dropped drastically when being a brother was no longer such a popular career and only seven men were living in the huge building.

St. Bonaventure had definitely outgrown its quarters in the basement of St. Bonaventure Church and needed room to grow. When a chance to buy the building presented itself, the school board of trustees jumped at it and here we were.

But buildings do not make a school, and we needed people to give it spirit and life and yes, success. I've only been here two years and only this year received the title of Dean of the Curriculum, heady sounding, but not all that glorious. I still have to teach three classes of social studies and do all the paper work the dean title carried.

Lee Castleberry is handsome, I'll give him that. He has that All American boy look with his dark blond hair with streaks of white from the sun, no doubt. His blue eyes were the color of a summer sky and his broad shoulders and narrow hips gave him an attractive physical appeal. But I still wonder how he is going to contribute to the making of the school. Good masculine looks don't make a school any more than a building.

Lee and Billy Bob joined the group at the table and the meeting proceeded. Lee said nothing at all, but since he was brand new, I didn't think much about that. At least, he wasn't going to be a know-it-all, talkative sort who tried to take over every faculty meeting. When Billy Bob announced Lee was the new football coach, I saw a scowl cross his face, but I don't think anyone else noticed. He kept the same non-committal look on his face, however, and offered no more input until the meeting broke up.

I went back to my office thinking of all the little things I had to do today and for the next several days to get the school year ready for the thousand little creatures who would soon be adding noise to these halls. It was still warm summer weather, and I thought a nice cold Coke would taste good before I got down to work. I hoped the delivery had been made for the drinks. I stepped out of my office into the hall and bumped right into Lee Castleberry. Was that luck or fate?

Billy Bob

Well, I finally have Lee here to work for me. I was afraid he'd turn me down, and I need him. He always made things happen in college. He's got the great brain and fortunately, he doesn't realize how intelligent and adaptable he is. That's to my advantage if I'm going to make something of this school—with his help. I remember in college how Lee always had the best ideas and then never took credit for them. Modest fellow. We all could use some of that. I never knew why he majored in journalism though except that he can write like Shakespeare and John Updike combined. That's always a help. As for me, I took the route for a degree in education because it was the simplest and easiest way. I don't like being in a class room, however. I like to be the leader and make the important decisions. It's scary here though. Too soon after integration. We can be selective in our choice of students since we aren't a public school. Being a church-related school, however, makes it our policy that all students are equal in the sight of God and that's as it should be. We accept anyone who can pass the admissions test.

With my two best friends, Lee and Grace to help, we can make this an outstanding school. Lee will do all the work, especially the dirty work, for me. People will listen to him, and I'll back his every idea.

Then there's Grace, the love of my life though she doesn't know it yet. A really intelligent woman appeals to me and with her close by, I can work my plan to have her fall head over heels for me and become my wife.

Wife. That's also a scary thought, but a headmaster at a prestigious school needs to be married. I can't be thought of as a crusty old bachelor, or heaven forbid, a homosexual or worse—some kind of pervert. A beautiful wife like Grace will complete my ambitions.

I guess the first thing we have to tackle is how to get the money to pay for this building. It suits our needs perfectly and the price is right. But we need the money and we need it fast.

They say the building is haunted. That will be handy for Halloween. I'll have to go up on the third floor and check out the ghost lodgings. Those tiny cells up there where the brothers lived ought to have some spirit left from their days there. Living in a space only about eight by six certainly cramps one's style. Nothing in there but a bed and a chest of drawers, and one lamp. How did they stand it?

All those internal walls will have to be removed and the building brought up to the present building and safety codes for schools. That will cost a ton of money. Maybe it is going to take longer to achieve my dreams than I planned. We'll have to lock the third floor for the first year. The inspectors say the building is safe enough but not up to code for having students above the second floor. And we need a new gym. The present one is little more than a stable—ha, a stable, that's fitting for a former religious order. Wonder if it has a manger?

I've got to call a meeting and settle some of these matters. The board of trustees for the school will have to give us some guidance. Better get Lee on the public relations right away and get out some press releases. Lee and Grace, we have to become the three musketeers and get this show on the road.

MARGARET BOLAND
The Meetings

"I suppose you wonder why I've called you here today," Billy Bob began with a chuckle.

The group around the table did not respond with even a single smile.

Billy Bob continued. "We have to arrange for financing for the purchase of this building. I'd like your ideas on how to do that."

"We could have a bake sale," Mary Anderson snickered. She was the librarian, or she would be when the area which had been used for a chapel by the brothers was cleared of its pews and shelves were installed.

"Good idea, Mary," Billy Bob responded, "but I'm not sure the bank would be willing to wait for all those cakes to bake."

"We need people on the board of trustees who have influence and money," Lee said.

"I agree with that. But how do we get them? The board pretty much picks their own members."

"Would they at least take our suggestions and recommendations?" Lee asked.

"They might," Billy Bob looked around the table.

There was a murmur of voices and Billy Bob finally cleared his throat and called for attention. "I'll go around the table and ask for each one of you for your opinion."

Since Lee was seated at Billy Bob's right, it fell to him to speak first. "As I said, we need influence and money people. I understand the school has just been incorporated as a separate entity from St. Bonaventure Church, but it will always be associated with the church. Why couldn't we get members of the vestry to sit on the school board and make the rector a member as well?"

Billy Bob stood up. "I think you've got it. By Jove, as Professor Higgins' friend said of Eliza Doolittle. By Jove, I think you've got it."

Lee continued. "There are men on the church vestry who are also bankers. It seems a perfect fit to me."

"Lee, old friend, I knew you'd come through for St. Bonnie. That is a splendid idea. I think we can adjourn this meeting and get right on that suggestion."

The group filed out of the room with most of them sighing

in relief that no more of their time would be spent on this particular situation.

"Lee," Billy Bob called. "I wonder if I can count on you to go over to the church and talk to the rector about this. After all, you have the PR charm and the way with words."

"So much for the football program," Lee growled.

Lee caught up with Grace in the hall. "About time for another Coke, isn't it?"

"I suppose you'll need it, however, they have moved the machine to the teachers' lounge. Do you know where that is? Come on, I'll show you."

A sofa and several comfortable chairs had been moved into a room near the chapel, which was going to become the library.

"All the comforts of home," Lee remarked as he looked around the room. There was a copy machine in place, a telephone, a work table with straight chairs surrounding it, and the Coke machine.

"My day to buy," Lee said and put coins into the red box.

They chose the sofa and sat down with their drinks.

"You have one tough job, Lee," Grace said. "I'm betting it isn't what you had in mind when you came to St. Bonaventure."

"Damn right it isn't. All I had in mind when I took this job was a steady paycheck and a chance to get some order in my life. Eating regularly comes to mind. And I wanted time to write my great American novel. And I certainly never imagined fund raising or football coaching to be a part of the deal."

"Oh, you'll do all right," Grace said. "I think you have the charm and know how to persuade the proverbial drowning man to grasp the anchor you throw him. Do you plan to go over and talk to the rector this afternoon?"

"Might as well, the sooner the better. I still have to get the football equipment inventoried and the schedule worked out. I've only been here one day and already I'm overwhelmed with work."

"Good luck," Grace said and put her drink can in the recycling container.

Lee walked the two blocks from the newly acquired school building to St. Bonaventure's Church, thinking as he walked on how he would approach the rector. He needn't have concerned himself. The rector, he was told by a secretary, was having visitations at the hospital and wouldn't be back until after five o'clock.

Lee told her he would come back in the morning.

"Could I tell him the nature of your visit?" the secretary asked.

"I suppose so. I want to talk to him about getting members of the vestry to serve on the new school board."

"You've come to the right person," she said. "Mr. Graham has been in favor of that since the school was first founded. Do come back and talk to him in the morning."

Lee passed a closed door as he left. It read "The Reverend Walter Graham, Jr."

Lee's meeting the next morning with the Reverend Mr. Graham was indeed fruitful. The rector immediately agreed to the idea and had several suggestions for new board members. "Jack Pratt will be a good one. I don't need to tell you what a lot of flack he takes with his name, but he's a good man. Then there's Marvin Byrd, he's the senior warden and president of the Gulf Coast National Bank. He knows how to handle money, that's for sure."

"Could I come to a vestry meeting and discuss this with them?"

"Next Monday night is the next scheduled regular meeting. I'll put you on the agenda and we'll take it from there."

Lee returned to his designated office under the stands at the gym. It was hot and sticky and still smelled like a locker room, but there was nothing to do but start counting helmets and jerseys and see what he needed to order to get the football program started. The boys were to report tomorrow which was already late because other schools had begun their practice on the first allowed day.

Lee racked his brain for how he'd handle the opening session with the boys. Since he knew so little of football strategy, he decided he would have to resort to pep talks and encouragement. With only three seniors, it was not likely that he would have any player who could set the mood.

He spent the rest of the afternoon on the telephone trying to get more football games scheduled. St. Bonnie would be in the smallest category of the state athletic association so he needed to stay in that category if they had any hope of winning any games. He decided to concentrate on other church supported and independent schools, and put in a call to Pass Christian, Mississippi for Coastal

Episcopal School. They agreed to a game the Saturday before Thanksgiving and Lee felt he was on the way.

The meeting with the vestry was equally rewarding. Both Lee's recommendations and those from the rector were accepted quickly and voted upon without any dissent.

The next general planning meeting for the school included the new people and got off to a quick and productive start.

Marvin Byrd, the banker spoke first. "We can get some of the capital in the form of a loan, but we need more collateral than the building, especially since we haven't made any substantial down payment."

"Would they take personal notes?" Lee asked.

"Personal notes? You mean personal loans or letters of credit written to the bank assuring them we'd repay the money." Marvin Byrd twirled the pen he held in his hand.

"What I mean is this." Lee said. "Let's show them how much we believe in this school by each signing a personal note for $10,000 guaranteeing the building loan."

"What an unusual idea," Billy Bob said. "Lee, I knew we could count on you for direction. I'll be the first to sign my personal note."

Marvin Byrd shook his head. "It's highly unusual. We have fifteen present here at this time. At $10,000 a personal note, we'd have $150,000, more than the loan on the building. Let me take this to the loan committee at the bank and see if they would be willing to agree to that. And I'll sign my note right now. It's unusual all right, but it just might work."

The remaining members of the board voiced approval and one by one, they each pledged the sum of $10,000.

Lee's internal thoughts were pure panic. Where on earth would he get $10,000 when he hadn't even got his first paycheck? But it was his idea and he had to lend his support or look like an utter fool. Well, it was only a pledge. He wouldn't be called upon to pay that sum unless the school reneged on their loan. Good management of the school income should provide for regular payments. He couldn't do anything else but sign the personal note.

The meeting hadn't taken as long as expected. Marvin Byrd walked out with Lee.

"I hear you're the new football coach," he said.

"That's right. I've been trying to get the schedule firmed up."

"My boy is in the eleventh grade—great quarterback. I know you'll see that he gets enough playing time to be looked at by some of the colleges for a possible scholarship. We're expecting great things of St. Bonaventure this year with all the expansion the school is doing. I must admit, however, I didn't expect our new football coach to be a financial expert. You had the perfect solution for the loan to be worked out. I hope the football season is as successful. "

"I hope so, too," Lee murmured. "I certainly hope so."

CHAPTER TWO

Lee Castleberry looked out over the group of boys who sat before him on the field of brown grass. Dust floated about the air after the group had run around a clay-packed oval that surrounded the area. The late summer heat was stifling and not a breath of air stirred. Even though it was mid-afternoon, the sun glared intensely and the temperature must have been near one hundred.

"Okay, fellows," Lee began. He wondered what he was going to say next. "We're here to form St. Bonaventure's first ever football team, right?"

There were a few half hearted "Yeahs" from some of the back row.

"We've got to get more enthusiasm than that into our team. We're forming St. Bonaventure's first ever football team, right?"

"Right." A few more voices were added.

"Louder!"

"Right!" The whole group finally responded.

"Then let's get to it."

And that's what they did for the next two hours pausing only for water breaks. Lee came back into his office wringing wet with sweat and aching in every muscle of his body. He plopped down in his desk chair which squeaked in protest. I'll have to oil this thing, Lee thought.

He reviewed his clipboard notes. There were a total of thirty one boys, hardly enough to field an offense and defense. If anybody got hurt, and that was inevitable, he'd be pushed to have enough players to put on the field.

He'd already picked out a couple of guys who he thought would be the glue on which he would hang the entire program. Charlie Morris was an eleventh grader who could throw the football three-fourth of the length of the field. The other players already showed him respect. Yes, he would be the team leader.

Second in command would be Marvin Byrd, another eleventh grader. The only senior who came out for practice was a thin, nerdy-looking, horn-rimmed glasses wearer named Benjamin Baker.

If the first day was the hardest, then at least this day was over. Lee went over to the main building and took a shower, where such facilities had been provided for the brothers. With no locker room, he guessed his football team would have to go home and shower after practice and games. Of one thing he was certain. He needed an assistant coach, maybe more than one extra person, to handle all the details of a football team. He'd prefer someone who knew what he was doing. Lee still felt very uncomfortable in this head coach position.

Lee went up to the second floor to seek Billy Bob and report on the first practice but no one was in his office. Lee walked on down the hall to Grace's office and found her sitting at her desk pouring over a stack of papers.

"How'd it go?" She looked up as Lee entered the room.

"It went." Lee said.

"Nothing else but it went?"

"I guess it was okay. I've got thirty one boys; but I'm not sure some of them can walk and chew gum, as the saying goes. And I'm not sure I can handle everything without some help. Do you think I dare ask Billy Bob for an assistant?"

"Sure. Ask him. Anybody knows a football team can't be run by just one person. Maybe you could get Allen Rogers to help. A science teacher should have some good ideas about football."

"Yeah, right, it's such a mind boggling activity. We could use some brawn more than brains, not only for coaching, but especially for the players."

"What are you planning to offer for the girls in the way of sports?"

"I wasn't planning to offer anything unless some of them want to join the football team. I'm not the athletic director, only the football coach."

"I wouldn't be too sure of that."

"Too sure of what?"

"That you're only the football coach."

When Lee finally caught up with Billy Bob, he found Grace was right. Billy Bob told him as soon as the football got started; he wanted a volleyball team for the girls to be set up.

"Come on, Billy Bob, be reasonable. I only took the football to help out. I can't take on volleyball, too."

"Sure you can," Billy Bob assured him. "Lee, you can do anything. Volleyball can't be that hard. And you don't have to coach it yourself. Get one of the women faculty members to take that job."

"I don't even know the women faculty members."

"Then you can meet them tomorrow when we have our first faculty meeting."

Lee studied the women at the faculty meeting the next day. He didn't see any likely prospects for coach, and when he asked that any interested faculty, men or women, stay after the meeting to talk about coaching volleyball, no one remained.

Grace came over to console the dejected Lee. "You look like you'd like to return to the land of public relations and journalism."

"What am I supposed to do? This whole school is nuts and I'm even crazier to stay here. Nothing is worth this. I'll go on the unemployment line. I'm being asked to do things I neither like nor understand. Things I haven't been trained to do. I want out of here. I'm not coming back tomorrow."

"You can't give up so soon," Grace said. "Things will work out. Maybe we can put out the word we're looking for a volleyball coach and hire somebody new."

"And pay them with what? You heard Billy Bob during the meeting saying how it would be necessary for us to operate within budget this first year in this new building and while we're establishing St. Bonaventure as a pillow of education in the community. You'll note I'm using his exact words. Words don't make things happen. People make things happen."

"I'll tell you what I'll do," Grace said. "Since it's important to me, and certainly to the school, for girls to have an athletic program, I'll meet with the players who want to play volleyball and get things started while you keep looking for a coach."

"You're willing to do that?"

"Yes."

"For me?"

"No, Lee, for the girls."

And so Grace Garland called a meeting of the girls who wanted to play volleyball. Fifty-three young ladies showed up for a sport which has six members on a team, enough for eight full teams with a few substitutes thrown in for good measure.

Grace did a daring thing. She set up four teams each with second teams and entered the four teams in a citywide YWCA tournament which was being held just before school started.

There was no money for uniforms for so many teams, so Grace arranged for each player to provide her own navy blue shorts and T-shirt of various colors denoting each team.

Some of the girls had previous experience playing volleyball, and Grace put them on the Blue team which actually managed to win several matches and advance in the draw until they met one of the best Catholic High School teams in the quarter finals.

The other teams weren't so outstanding but the Reds won a match, and the Whites advanced with a default. The Gold team could never get their act together. They were the youngest of the groups, mostly made up of seventh graders. They lost the first match they played but their interest remained high, and Grace stated that they were an upcoming group to watch for future success.

Grace called the parents of every child who played in that volleyball tournament to tell them their daughter was appreciated, that she had contributed to the reputation of the team and the school and that great things were expected in the future.

"And I thought I was the one who was public relations director." Lee said to Grace as they discussed the results of the tournament in her office the following week.

"You know as well as I do that we have to start some place," Grace said. "If we get the parents rallying behind what we are trying to accomplish, we're half way there."

"That shouldn't be hard with football the religion of the South," Lee said. "But the difference is that in football, you are supposed to win. Let a coach lose two or three games and everyone is screaming for his head, for him to be replaced."

"There's an easier task we have to perform," Grace said. "We have to get a team mascot picked. Any ideas about that?"

"Maybe we should have a student body election."

"Good idea. That way whatever mascot is picked, it can't be said anyone dictated we insult American Indians, or some poor animal, or any ethnic bodies."

"We need to do this right away. The first football game is

only two weeks off and we can't be labeled the Nobody Team. That would wreck the morale, that is if there is any morale to start with."

The election was set up and students voted on the school mascot, the colors for the teams, and the name for the new school newspaper. Lee had found out to his dismay that he had still another duty as PR director, that of starting a school newspaper which would be produced by a class Lee would teach called aptly, Journalism. He was finally being assigned something he knew how to do, Lee thought.

Lee and Grace sat in his office with the piles of ballots they were going to count. They promised election results at the assembly to be held the next morning so the job had to be completed this afternoon.

They arranged the ballots in stacks for the mascot first. From the start, it was obvious that a group had been active in promoting the mascot name "The Bulls". It became even more obvious that the name would win.

"We can't allow this," Grace said. "We simply can't call the girls' teams the Bulls."

"You're right," Lee agreed. "But what can we do? The majority wins in America, remember?"

"We should have known better than to put this out for an election in an immature student body. But this mascot name is going to last long after the present students finally mature, if indeed they ever do, and leave the school. We have to do something here. What name seems to be second?"

"Hard to tell. Here's an interesting one, the Bonnie Blues."

"Great and can't you see the boys playing under that name."

They shuffled through the ballots again.

"It looks like the Saints name is running a close second," Lee pulled a pile of ballots to one side.

"St. Bonaventure Saints," Grace said. She leaned back in her chair and repeated the name. "I like that. I think it would work."

"Then let's announce the Saints has won," Lee gathered the papers. "No one will ever know otherwise."

"What if someone asks for a recount?" Grace asked.

"Hmmmmm. That could pose a problem. The boys pushing the Bulls name have probably already made a count among themselves."

"But we can't let the Bulls win."

"Agreed. But neither can we afford a recount." Lee sat back in his chair and thought. He made a steeple with his fingers and leaned back.

"I've got it," he said. "Let's put the ballots in today's trash, only someone might go through the trash and find them. We'll really have to go out and burn them. We can always say they were put in the trash in error and if they can't be found, the trash must have been picked up last night.."

"Yes, discarded in error, the error of the vote. We might even get picked to count presidential votes in the future" Grace pondered the thought and smiled. "It really isn't ethical to throw them away, but when the ox is in the ditch, something drastic must be done."

"We can do that and announce the Saints won. Or, we can say the Bulls won, which they did, and suggest that isn't a good name and have a free for all the rest of the week. Or, we can call for a new election for which there isn't time and for which there is no evidence that the outcome would be any different. And finally, we need the mascot name by in the morning."

The two sat quietly.

Grace looked at Lee and smiled. "You'll be a good public relations director among other things." She scooped up the files of ballots. "Got a match?"

Lee got up every morning determining that this would be his last day at St. Bonaventure. He just wasn't happy. This wasn't what he wanted to do with his life. Teaching school had been something he always avoided and said he would never do. And here he was doing it.

He thought of many things as he was shaving. The thing that kept him going back was not his friendship with Billy Bob. In fact, Billy Bob had been more distant in the past few days. He was hard to catch in his office and he seemed bored and offered no solutions when Lee tried to tell him of the problems he was encountering.

"You can figure it out, Lee, ole boy," he'd say, and then turn his attention to a phone call or some paper on his desk as a way of dismissing Lee.

The first football game was a disaster and the newly named

Saints lost 55-6 to a nearby Catholic parochial school. Lee tried to cheer the team when the contest finally ended.

"We're just getting started," he said to them. "We'll do better and
we'll get better. We all have to work harder. You'll see. We'll win some games."

But they didn't win any games and after the third loss, Billy Bob called Lee into his office.

"The football team doesn't seem to be getting off the ground," Billy Bob said.

"Give us a chance. I've got guys on the team who have never played organized football, and we're playing schools that have raised gridiron prodigies since they were six years old."

"Excuses only satisfy those who make them, Lee," Billy Bob continued, "But we have to build this program quicker. I'm getting you some help."

"Help?"

"Yes, an assistant coach. There's a board member, Tom Thompson, who has a son who will come this afternoon to help with the football team. The son's name is Tony. I hope you'll welcome him."

"He'll be more than welcomed. Trying to handle thirty-one boys and teach offense and defense it more than one person can handle."

"Good," Billy Bob said. "That will give you time for another assignment. I want you to develop a public relations program that will project the aims of St. Bonaventure. We have to let the public know we are no longer the little school in the church basement, that we will have a full high school by the end of this year, and that our high school is coed. Got it?"

"I hear what you are saying. A program to develop an image like that will take time, I mean several years."

"Then you'd better get started hadn't you?"

"Let me see if I have this right. We will be a full high school since we are adding the twelfth grade this year. Will we be accredited?"

Billy Bob sighed. "You don't have to push that point just yet. We have applied for accrediting by the state and the Southern Association, but a lot of things have to be accomplished and inspection teams must come in and observe. We'll be accredited all right. With Grace handling the curriculum that won't be a problem, just a matter of time."

"I see. Then I'll concentrate on the coed."

"Yes, that's important because our biggest rival, as you well know, is the boys' military school across town. Military schools are on the way out. It's not the trend anymore especially since the Vietnam War. And, of course, military schools aren't coed. We have a student body now that's top heavy with girls, so we need to balance it out and be a truly coed institution."

"That still leaves the little school in the church basement."

"Look Lee, I've told you what I want you to do. It's your job to get busy and do it. I'm not telling you how to do it. You're the public relations expert. Just go do it, okay?"

The telephone on Billy Bob's desk rang at that moment and Lee got up and left.

As he walked down the hall, he began to wonder why Billy Bob had hired him in the first place. Was it because he felt sorry that Lee had no job? No, not likely. Was it because he really needed and wanted a PR person for the school? Possibly. And he certainly couldn't have hired anyone else for that position who would have worked for the salary Lee was being paid. Was it to do the dirty work for Billy Bob? Lee felt he was getting closer to the answer with that question. Even back in college, Billy Bob always liked to push ideas and then take the credit. He had often urged Lee to tackle something difficult and controversial, and then when it didn't work out, Billy Bob would point out the fallacy of the operation and how Lee should have done it differently. But when such a plan succeeded, Billy Bob took all the credit, claiming it was his idea from the beginning.

That's it, thought Lee. He wants me to take all the chances and then he can get all the glory—or place all the blame. He comes out Scott free either way. Ole Billy Bob never changes.

If that's the way he wants it, then that's the way we'll play it, Lee decided. He went to his office to think of a news release that could begin his new PR program.

The computer he had been promised had not been delivered yet. This annoyed Lee and he went to the computer lab to find a machine to use. A class was in session and there were no empty places in the room which only had ten computers to start with.

Just how am I supposed to be a public relations director with nothing to type on, he fumed. He went to Grace's office and found it empty. Then he remembered this was the period she taught social studies. Her computer sat empty with the screen saver dancing across the screen.

I'll just sit here and compose my news release, thought Lee, and pulled up a chair.

He felt a little uncomfortable using someone else's computer, but he needed to write the release before it was time for football practice. He determined he would ease more and more of the football duties to Tony Thompson and free up more time for himself. Then the same old thought came back to him. I don't have to come back here tomorrow.

Grace came in just as the final page of the news release was coming from her printer.

"You might have asked," Grace said as she closed the door behind her.

"I know that. And I'm sorry. Billy Bob wanted a news release out as soon as possible and my computer hasn't been delivered. I hope you don't mind." He got up and moved aside so Grace could sit at her desk.

"It's okay, just tell me next time you plan to use my computer. Let me see the news release."

Lee handed her the two page item.

Grace read it quickly, then looked up. "Big push for the coed, eh?"

"Boss's orders. Only that's just the first third. I have to incorporate the high school development and get rid of the image of the little school in the church basement."

"This sounds fine. I guess nobody told you that getting a computer for your office isn't in the budget. You'll have to usc the computer lab."

"I can't do that. The place is always full. They have a class nearly every period."

"Let me know how you solve it," Grace said. "Now if you'll excuse me, I have some work to do."

"I know how to solve it," Lee muttered as he turned to leave, "I just won't come back in the morning."

He stormed down the hall to his office planning to gather his belongings and be out of there. Well, maybe after football practice. He couldn't leave the team like that. He'd ease control over to Tony, then he could leave.

Lee opened the office door to find Ben Baker sitting at his desk working on a laptop computer.

"Hello, Ben," Lee said. "Catching up on some school work?"

"Not really, Coach, I'm working on a program to keep statistics for the football team. You know, yards gained, tackles, punt distance, all that stuff."

Lee paused before answering. "That's great, Ben. I'm sorry I didn't think of that myself. That will be very helpful in getting our stories in the sports section of the local paper. In fact, as of this minute, I'm putting you in charge of statistics. Can you get me some print outs today?"

"I'll have to put the stuff on disk and go to the computer lab to print it. I don't have a printer yet. It's bad enough carrying this laptop around."

An idea flashed into Lee's head. "That will be fine. And Ben, why don't you leave your laptop here on my desk. You can come in and use it anytime. It's pretty quiet in here."

"Gee, Coach, that would be great. You sure you wouldn't mind?"

"Of course not, Ben, you'll be helping me and the team, and since I don't have a computer yet, would you mind if I typed some news releases on it—when you aren't using it, of course?"

"Help yourself. I'm so relieved I won't have to haul the laptop around anymore. It takes up all the room in my backpack and it's heavy."

Football practice went very well that afternoon. Tony was a genius with new plays and had lots of helpful suggestions for both offense and defense. He had even brought in a sophomore who was a well known soccer player who agreed to play on the team if he could kick.

Lee went back to his office as the sun was setting thinking maybe he'd wait one more day before not coming back. He passed the janitor who was pushing a hand truck with a printer on it.

"What's that you've got there, LeRoy?" Lee asked.

"Extra printer. It isn't working so they told me to take it back to storage. If it ain't working, why don't they just throw it away. We got too much stuff taking up room in storage anyway. I don't even have room to keep my chemicals for the cleaning the floors."

"Tell you what, LeRoy, just put the printer in my office. I have room for it and maybe I can even get it fixed."

LeRoy smiled. "Yes, sir, I can do that."

The next day Lee approached Ben about the printer.

"They say it's broken, Ben, but I thought maybe you could look at it and see what's wrong with it."

Ben tinkered with the printer about thirty minutes over at the make shift desk Lee had set up with an old table and a folding chair. He fed paper into the printer, hit buttons and opened the cover from time to time.

"Got it," Ben stated. "It was just this little sensor in the back where the paper feeds. It had got off track and didn't recognize a new sheet. I think it will work fine now. Shall I take it back somewhere?"

"You don't have to do that, Ben. And you won't have to go to the computer lab to print anymore. We, or rather you, just got us a printer."

"That will save us lots of time, Coach. Now I won't have to run back and forth to the lab. I can do even more stats and maybe help you do some other stuff as well."

After Ben left, Lee tilted back in his chair. It nearly fell over as the back spring was too loose. He caught himself just before tumbling backward. This day had turned out better than it started, he thought. Help with the football, a soccer-style kicker for the team, a computer and printer and a nerd operator for his office alone. Yes, he'd come back one more day and see what happened.

CHAPTER THREE

The crisp air of fall had finally come to St. Bonaventure's campus. The leaves of Old Annie were yellow and red, making a glorious banner of color for the entrance drive that led to the main building.

The football team had finally won a game 7-6 on the strength of the kicking leg of the soccer-style kicker, Martin Rooney. Lee had almost forgotten to ponder whether or not he would go back the next morning. With his assistant coach, the football had gotten easier and he was actually enjoying writing up some of the press releases he was developing for the three-pronged approach to changing the image of the school.

The arrival of fall and the slanted yellow light of the sun made Lee think of Thanksgiving, which was, he had decided, his favorite holiday. It was a relaxing holiday, none of the Christmas rush and hectic planning. He wanted to spend the holiday with his parents and other relatives, but with only a four day weekend, he would spend two of those days just driving. His budget wouldn't allow flying and his car probably wouldn't make the trip without at least two new tires.

No, he concluded, he would cook Thanksgiving dinner and ask Grace to come join him. He knew she wasn't planning any out of town trip because he had heard her tell Billy Bob she was going to enjoy the holiday at home watching some football games and maybe getting out her Christmas card list and starting on it.

Lee found himself looking for Grace every morning. The very sight of her cheered his day. She was so beautiful and so intelligent and he admired her very much. He'd just finished a press release announcing she was dean of academic affairs for St. Bonnie. Nothing about her job description had changed, her duties and salary would be the same, but Billy Bob thought the new title had an academic ring to it and directed Lee to prepare the news release.

Lee spent more time on the writing of this item than any other he'd written. He wanted it to be perfect, just as Grace was perfect. He even took her picture to the newspaper, but they declined to run it with the story. He tried for television coverage, but the local stations were more interested in the football statistics than they were the announcement of a new dean of academic affairs. Maybe one day he could announce a new athletic director and gets lots of coverage and spend more of his time doing things he enjoyed more than coaching football.

The team was not without a crisis—one even greater than the losing season. They only won one game. The final game was played Friday night before the upcoming Thanksgiving holiday week. They lost to the smaller Episcopal Gulf Coast School—the very one Lee had picked as a certain win. The score was 14-0 and the team hadn't played very well and came away depressed at ending the season like that.

Lee was closing up things in his office and the athletic store room when Ben came in. Lee remembered that Ben had played only about five minutes and had not distinguished himself in that time—in fact he had missed a tackle and allowed the Coast team to make a first down–one of many they made that night.

"Hi Coach," Ben began. "I was wondering if I could stay in the office awhile and do some of the statistics."

"I suppose so, but don't you want to go out with the team for the after game festivities." He couldn't say celebration for it was anything but that.

"I'd really rather catch up on this stuff and wrap up the season that is if you don't mind."

"No, of course I don't mind. I hope you aren't expecting me to stay with you. I want to get home. Would you lock up when you finish?"

"Sure, Coach, thanks a lot."

Lee left wondering why it was so urgent to get the stats done tonight. He found out later. A phone call about 12:30 a.m. informed him that the police had rounded up a number of St. Bonaventure students who had been caught for underage drinking at one of the local pubs. The police officer who called him indicated Lee needed to come down to the station and supervise the release of the boys to their parents.

Lee fumed as he threw on some clothes and left his apartment. How stupid can you be, he thought. What on earth were they thinking? Hadn't he told them after the game that the season had been a success in that they finally had a football team? They had won one game and they had the beginnings of a great tradition to look forward to.

Drinking beer? Damn. He wondered if some of them had been driving after the beers as well. Some of them weren't even old enough to have a drivers' license. This wasn't in his job description, but then hardly anything he did was in his job description.

It was near three a.m. when Lee got back home. He'd called parents and assisted the police with the necessary reports. Most of the parents were pretty upset, not only at being called out in the middle of the night, but mostly because their sons had been caught drinking beer. .

If Lee had thought the boys were dejected at the end of the game, it was nothing beside their present attitude. He couldn't help but notice, however, that they were much more upset at getting caught than they were for drinking the suds.

What Lee wasn't prepared for was Billy Bob's lecture on Monday morning. "How could you let them do that?" he began.

"How could I?" Lee protested. "I knew nothing about the whole thing till I got the call from the police."

"You should have anticipated it. You're the coach. You knew they were upset for the loss, for the whole season, for that matter. You should have supervised them and seen to it that they got home safely."

"Come on, Billy Bob, get real. Those boys are teenagers. I can't and shouldn't be responsible for their conduct. Why didn't their parents see that they got home and in bed safely?"

"The parents sent their children to us for education and for character development. It's part of our job to carry out that responsibility. You should have seen they got home."

"Will that be all?" Lee clinched his teeth and drew his mouth into a tight line.

"Yes, just don't let it happen again."

"The football season is over, thank God," Lee muttered under his breath as he turned and left the room. He resisted the impulse to slam the door behind him.

"I'm not coming back in the morning," Lee said aloud as he walked down the hall. He wanted to stop in Grace's office and vent his feelings but he decided he'd better let his anger cool before talking to her.

He went on back to his office. Ben was bent over the laptop, pounding keys.

"Have you been here all weekend?" Lee asked.

"No, sir. I didn't stay much longer after you left Friday night." Ben hung his head lower

"Is something the matter, Ben?"

"No, Coach—yes, Coach, there is something the matter."

"Do you want to talk about it?"

"I guess so."

After a long period of silence, Lee finally said, "Do you want to talk about it now?"

"I don't know how to start."

"Try at the beginning."

"Well, Coach, the thing is, I knew where the boys were going Friday night after the game. I didn't want to go with them, but I couldn't tell them that. So I told them I had to get the stats done, and that's why I wanted to stay here in the office."

Lee blew out his breath. "I wish you'd told me the real reason Friday night."

"Gee, Coach, I couldn't do that. You know that would be ratting on the gang. It's bad enough they call me a 'nerd'. At least being on the team has helped them treat me nicer. But to rat on them, that would have been suicide for me."

"I suppose you're right." Lee sat down at his desk. "Well, do you have the stats ready?"

"Yes, sir," Ben swept up a handful of papers and gave them to Lee. "I guess you won't be needing me anymore."

Lee thought of the laptop. He'd be lost without having it in his office. And, he felt sorry for Ben. He was a good kid and smart as a whip.

He turned to the young man. "We will certainly need your expertise for the basketball season coming up. Do you think you could work up some software that would keep shooting stats, total game points per player, percentage of shots made? All that sort of thing."

"Yes, I can do that. I've already been thinking about such a program. I'll finish it up and test it before the season starts if that's all right with you."

"That will be fine. Just leave your laptop here and work on

it whenever you want to."

"I will, Coach. And thanks for understanding."

Lee wasn't sure whether he understood or not, but Ben was no bother in the office and he, Lee, did need that computer.

When school let out, Lee decided to go to the grocery store and buy the items for Thanksgiving dinner. He planned how he would ask Grace the next morning first thing.

Picking out a turkey was easy. Deciding what weight was needed was more a problem. Finally, Lee decided with only the two of them a ten pound bird would be sufficient. He bought some sweet potatoes, cranberry sauce in a can, some salad makings, and as he was picking up a package of rolls, he decided he would make cornbread instead. He was thankful his mother had showed him many pointers about cooking and how to prepare a number of good dishes. He'd make the cornbread tonight and save some for making cornbread dressing.

He picked out a bottle of Pinot Grigio, decided on a pre-baked pecan pie and finished off his list with chips and some dip. That should do it, he thought, and felt smug about his plans.

He and Grace would enjoy a nice dinner about noon, or maybe even in the afternoon. He'd pick some romantic music to add to the atmosphere, or if she preferred, they could watch whatever traditional college football game was on television.

The next morning, bright and early, Lee went to Grace's office to ask her to come for dinner. She wasn't there. Where could she be? She didn't have an early morning class. He was eager to have her confirm she'd be coming for dinner. He should have asked her earlier, he thought. But it was only Tuesday, and Thanksgiving was still two days away.

It was nearly school dismissal time when Lee finally saw Grace coming across the campus from the parking lot.

"I've been looking for you all day," Lee said.

"I had a meeting with the finance committee down at the bank," Grace said. "If we're going to get accredited by the Southern Association, we have to offer a few more subjects and that means hiring some more instructors for second semester. Can you teach algebra?" She laughed.

"Yes, I could. My minor is in mathematics, but don't tell his highness or he'll give me the job of doing that, too."

"Are you really that unhappy here, Lee?"

"Off and on. Some days I really think I just can't come back in the morning. But my happiness will be greatly increased if you'll come to dinner Thanksgiving Day. I'm fixing everything traditional."

"I would have never guessed you to be a cook," Grace nodded and looked at Lee.

"I'm pretty good at it. In fact I might be a better cook than I am a school teacher, and I might be happier at it."

"Things will get better here. You'll see." Grace smiled.

"Then it's settled. You'll come for dinner, say about one, and then we'll eat whenever we want to after that."

"Lee, I'd love to come. I wish you'd asked me sooner. But you see, his highness, as you choose to call him, asked me last Friday to have Thanksgiving dinner with him, so I can't come to your house. But thanks anyway for thinking of me and for asking."

CHAPTER FOUR

Lee woke up Thanksgiving morning wondering where he was in his life and more than that, where he was going. Grace had asked him if he was that unhappy. He wasn't as unhappy as he was discontented. I would have been much happier if Grace had come to Thanksgiving dinner here, he thought.

He got up and put on a pot of coffee and wondered how to spend the day. He'd call his mother and wish her a happy holiday. There was all this food he'd bought. He guessed he might as well cook the turkey as it was too big to put in his freezer.

He got it in the oven and sat drinking a second cup of coffee. It was time to make some decisions. He'd fulfill his contract with Billy Bob. That's a joke, he thought. He had no written contract with either Billy Bob or the school. It was all a verbal agreement, dependent on the integrity of the parties involved. He couldn't quit until the year was out. He couldn't live with himself if he did that. He concluded that there was nothing to do but make the most of it.

The smell of the roasting turkey soon filled the apartment with a delightful aroma. Lee looked out the window and saw a bunch of children kicking a soccer ball back and forth. He thought idly that St. Bonaventure needed to have a soccer team. They would probably do a lot better in sports where physical size was not the criteria it was in football. Unless St. Bonnie got some turnip-green-fed giants, their football team would never be able to compete with the public schools who gathered in all the local country boys.

He turned on his stereo and played a record of themes from movies. As the day wore on, he assembled some other dishes to go with the turkey. He calculated how long it should cook at the low oven temperature he'd set it on. He remembered his mother saying that if turkey was cooked a long time at a low temperature, it would be moist and tender. Whatever you say, Mom.

He made the call to his family and found everyone to be happy and in good health but wishing he could be there with them. He wished now that he had made the drive after all. He promised to be there for the Christmas holidays.

Since that was the only thing he had on his to-do list, Lee sat in his recliner and flipped through the newspaper. He couldn't remember being at such loose ends. He'd put too much emphasis on Grace coming. That was poor planning on his part, not to ask her sooner. Going to Billy Bob's of all things. He resented Billy Bob more for that than for any of the unmentioned jobs he'd thrust on Lee since his arrival at St. Bonaventure.

Lee dozed off in the comfortable chair and fell asleep. The ringing of the doorbell woke him with a start. Who on earth would be coming to his apartment on this day at this time? Probably a neighbor wanting to borrow an egg or something, he thought and got up and went to the door.

Lee's was totally startled when he opened the door and saw Grace standing there.

Finally he managed to say, "Hello, won't you come in?"

"I was hoping you'd be here," Grace said. "Is my invitation still open? Smells like the turkey is cooking for somebody."

Lee smiled broadly. "You bet the invitation is still open. I was just sitting here in my pity pot fretting that I had no one to eat the turkey with. I'm delighted to see you. I won't even ask why the sudden change in your plans. Come on in and I'll break open the jug of wine."

Lee was so excited over the arrival of Grace he could barely open the wine bottle, and he nearly knocked the wine glasses into the sink. They clattered together as he caught them.

Grace came into the kitchen. "What can I do to help?"

"Nothing, but make yourself at home. Everything can be ready in a few minutes. I'm afraid I didn't make the cornbread dressing, however, when I thought you weren't coming."

"Whatever you have planned and prepared will be fine," Grace took her glass of wine he had poured.

"Let's take our wine in the living room and enjoy it. Then I'll get the food on the table."

They sat down on the sofa. Lee lifted his glass and said, "To Thanksgiving. To us spending Thanksgiving together."

"I'll drink to that," Grace said and raised her glass.

"Thanksgiving is not a day to be spent alone," Lee said. "I'm so glad you're here."

"I suppose I owe you an explanation," Grace said. She leaned back and looked at Lee. "I guess you could say I got stood up."

"Billy Bob stood you up?"

"Whatever. I got to his house at the appointed time and he was getting ready to go out. He said he knew I'd understand, but at the last minute he got a call from the chairman of the board of trustees for the school inviting him to dinner at his house."

"That's terrible. Of course he should have turned that invitation down," Lee said. He was thinking he was glad Billy Bob didn't turn it down, but kept that thought to himself.

"I wasn't exactly pleased," Grace said. "But he said with the political angle of the invitation, he couldn't turn it down. He said he needed the chairman's support, and it would be rude to turn down such an invitation."

"Like it wasn't rude to leave you standing there with no dinner table to go to."

"But I have one," Grace smiled. "I'm here. And I get a distinct feeling that I am very welcomed here. You wouldn't leave me standing to go eat with the chairman of the board, would you?"

"Absolutely not."

They lingered over dinner for a long time and after the pecan pie, returned to the living room to finish the bottle of wine. Daylight saving time had gone off a few weeks before and it was dark early in the evening these days.

"Grace, I don't want to talk shop, but I'm concerned about the direction of my life at St. Bonaventure. Before you arrived today, I had decided to finish out the year because I've made the commitment, but after that, I'm out of here."

"That's noble and so like you to finish what you started. But I agree, if you don't like what you're doing, you should look for something else."

Lee found himself wishing Grace would stay in his house, in his life, forever. He thought he'd better move carefully now. He didn't want to scare her away with any forward movement or any words that might upset her.

"This is my favorite holiday," Lee finally said. "It's a day of peace and relaxation. It's a day to spend with those who are important in your life."

"Am I important in your life, Lee?" Grace asked.

"As a matter fact, yes, you are extremely important. In fact, if you weren't at St. Bonaventure, in spite of my honorable intention to fulfill my un-written contract, I would have been long gone way back about the second day."

"I'm glad you said that," Grace said. She moved closer to Lee and put her arm around his neck. "I didn't want to put you on the spot by making a move on you. I might not stay at St. Bonnie either if you weren't there."

Lee felt his face warming, his whole body heating up. "Why don't you just plan to spend the night?" he asked softly. "You really shouldn't be driving after drinking all the wine we've consumed."

Lee was absolutely flabbergasted and delighted when Grace never left. Together they watched the sun come up the next morning.

* * * *

The Monday morning after the holidays, Lee felt glorious, yet cautious. He had heard all about romance on the job and the dangers it presented. Grace had ended staying the whole weekend and they talked and made love and talked some more.

Anyone who ever wondered about the passion of women school teachers didn't know what they were talking about. Grace was glorious in bed as indeed she was out of bed, Lee thought.

They would get married. Christmas would be a lovely time for a wedding. He could take her to meet his parents and other family members. They could start the New Year as Mr. and Mrs. Lee Castleberry. He sighed and reveled at that thought.

The students would soon catch on that something was sparking between Lee and Grace. Kids weren't dumb and they were especially tuned in to personal relationships even if they hadn't learned how to handle them yet. Did anybody ever learn to handle relationships?

Lee determined that he and Grace would have to be very careful and very professional during school hours. What about after hours? Someone was bound to see her coming and going from his apartment. Well, they were adults and that was their business.

All that Monday, Lee remained in a daze thinking about the weekend the happiness it had brought him.

"You must have had a great Thanksgiving," Ben said to Lee as he came in to do his computer work.

"You're right, I did," Lee said and slapped Ben on the back. "I decided I had a lot to be thankful for this year, and I really enjoyed the day and the week end."

There was a lull in sports activity from Thanksgiving to Christmas holidays. Football and volleyball seasons were over, basketball practice had started, but Lee was relieved he did not have any participation in that sport. He was glad, not only because he didn't want to coach basketball, but because his observations about the student body were even more valid in round ball than in football. The tallest player St. Bonnie had was only about five feet, ten. If they were going to be a factor in the basketball scene in the city, they would have to find some tall fellows who could shoot the baskets.

But Lee was happy now and it showed in his attitude. He hoped no one was aware of why, most of all, Lee didn't want Billy Bob to know of his relationship with Grace.

Thanks to you, Billy Bob, thought Lee, I got my girl.

He decided to approach Billy Bob about a soccer team, however. Billy Bob agreed it was a good idea, but pointed out there was no budget for the sport.

"All we need is a ball," Lee reminded him. "We can make some goals with some two by fours. I found some old tennis nets in the store room which we can put into the frames."

"Then go to it," Billy Bob said. "But remember this was your idea and don't accuse me of giving you new jobs to oversee."

"I'll remember that," Lee said and got up and let the office.

He went straight to Grace's office. "Billy Bob has okayed the soccer team," he told her.

"Good. Maybe I'll get a group of girls and form a team and we can coach together," Grace said.

"Anything we do together will be wonderful," Lee said.

He wanted to move in and take Grace in his arms but he knew he couldn't. There would be so many times when he wanted to do that, he thought, and he wouldn't be able to.

But thank God for small blessings. No, thank God for great blessings. He smiled and left Grace's office.

CHAPTER FIVE

Lee wondered if Billy Bob was always going to start the faculty meetings with his inane remark, "I'm sure you wonder why I called you here."

That's what he'd just said and laughed at his own remark. There was a small smattering of snickers among the faculty.

"We're approaching Christmas holidays," Billy Bob went on. "It's essential that we keep our motion going forward. We're off to a good first semester, but once we return in January, we'll go into the mid-winter doldrums. It will take a lot of effort on your part to keep up the morale, to keep the students happy, and most of all, to please the parents."

Lee digested the last few words of Billy Bob's remarks. Isn't the love of learning supposed to keep students happy? What a joke. If more of them came here wanting to learn, we wouldn't have any problem.

Lee focused his attention to Billy Bob's remarks again.

"One very important thing," he slowed and put emphasis on each word. "We must have a faculty of the highest integrity. We must never let any word or rumor about our faculty reflect on anything but the most sterling moral character. Joseph, our music department head, has agreed and volunteered to stop playing the piano at a local night club bar, Joe, we appreciate your willingness to give up this second source of income in the better interest of St. Bonaventure. As for the rest of you, please be aware of the image you project to the public and let there be no reason for any gossip about the activities of any faculty member of this institution."

What's he driving at? Lee thought. Is he putting restrictions on the freedom of the faculty to live their lives as they see fit? His thoughts went immediately to his relationship with Grace. Did Billy Bob know about that? If so, why didn't he call the two of them in and privately suggest they not be obvious with their sudden interest in each other? But there had been no outward indication that they had any relationship. What in the world brought this on?

Grace, he would later find out, had similar thoughts. As they sat together in the lunch room with monitor duty, she spoke without looking at Lee.

"We've got to stop meeting like this."

Lee didn't look at her either. "Yes, these dark shadows out of sight of everyone are dangerous."

"No, I'm serious," Grace smiled and nodded to a student who passed the table.

"You heard what Billy Bob said. We have to be models of sainthood."

The bell rang at that moment starting the next class and the lunch room became a din of noise as students shuffled from tables, grabbed up book bags and left the cafeteria.

Grace started for the door.

"Wait, Grace," Lee urged. "What are you suggesting we do that is different from what we've been doing?"

"We just can't see each other anymore, that's what."

"That's crazy. The school can't dictate our personal lives."

"Of course it can. And we aren't just having a friendly little dating relationship, you know. All it would take for both of us to be toast would be for one person to report we'd been spending the night at each other's place. We just can't take the gamble, Lee. I can' afford to lose this job. And you can't either."

She hurried down the hall leaving Lee staring after her.

The week of the Christmas holidays came without Grace changing her thoughts about their life after school hours.

Finally, the day before the holidays were to begin, Lee went to Grace's office and shut the door behind him. He held up his hand to Grace indicating she was not to come behind him and open the door again.

"We've got to talk," he said. "I'd hoped to have you accompany me home for the holidays, introduce you to my folks, have a relaxing and happy time together during the holidays. Will you go with me?"

"Lee, you know I can't do that."

"Give me one good reason why you can't. You've already told me you can't go home again though you didn't say why. I'm not prying into why you don't want to go home; I just want you to go home with me."

"We can't talk about it here or now," Grace got up and opened the door.

"Then I'll come over to your house tonight. We have to settle this. I can't go on with all this secrecy and our not seeing each other."

"I'm going to dinner with Billy Bob tonight," Grace said matter-of-factly.

"You're what?"

"You heard me. I'm going to dinner with Billy Bob."

"I see. And just what does this mean?"

"It means go on to your own office right now. You can come to my place tomorrow night, if you must, but tonight is taken."

"You'd better hope he doesn't stand you up again for a member of the board."

Lee left with his thoughts boiling.

That night Lee imagined the worst of scenarios with Grace and Billy Bob at dinner. Was he being shot out of the saddle entirely? Why go out with Billy Bob? Maybe it was school business, but if so, couldn't it be handled during school hours? He had planned on packing for his holiday trip, but without Grace, he had no interest in that. He wasn't even looking forward to the Christmas holidays any more. This whole experience at St. Bonaventure had been nothing but a mistake from the start. He had finally found a woman he thought he could live with the rest of his life and the damn school was telling them they couldn't even see each other.

Well, tomorrow night would be Lee's last chance to plead his case for Grace to go with him, he thought. Wednesday was a half day at school allowing for an early start on Christmas holidays.

On impulse Tuesday night Lee stopped and bought a bouquet of flowers from the grocery store he passed en route to Grace's. He thrust them at her when she opened the front door.

"Thanks, Lee, you didn't have to do this."

"No, I didn't, and I don't have to do this, but I must." He stepped in, closed the door behind him, and took Grace in his arms. She did not resist.

"Oh, Lee, I don't know what to do." She took him by the hand and led him to the sofa where both sat down.

"Billy Bob is putting pressure on me."

"How is that?"

"He's found out something about my past life and telling me it could jeopardize my position at St. Bonaventure."

"He knows about us?"

"No, not that. Worse. Not that I mean our relationship is bad. Lee, I've worked years to get a position like I have, dean of academic affairs. If Billy Bob carries out his treat to make certain things public, I'm sure I'd have to resign; and then I'd have a terrible time getting any position again, let alone one this prestigious."

"Do you want to tell me the deep dark secret?"

"No, because then one more person would know. I'd like to forget it, but I can't and heaven knows, I do need a friend right now."

"Whatever have you done that is so terrible?"

Grace looked at Lee with tears in her eyes. "It's not what I've done. You see, Lee, my mother is in prison."

Lee leaned back and let out his breath. Inwardly, he was relieved. At least Grace hadn't had a child out of wedlock, robbed a bank, or embezzled the cheerleaders' bake sale funds."

"Do you want to tell me about it?" Lee asked.

"It began years ago," Grace said. "My father was very abusive. At least once a week, he would knock her down, do physical violence of some sort. And every day he was verbally abusive. I can barely remember his ever saying a kind word to her."

"Where were you living at the time?"

"We were in Kansas, a long way from Alabama, that's why I thought I could work in this state without the story following me."

"Anyway, this went on for years. I was too young at the time to know what to do. I would hide in the closet, but I could still hear him yelling at her and battering her around."

"It must have been awful."

"It was. He never touched us children, at least not for awhile. Then one night he came home drunk. He stormed into the kitchen where my mother and I were fixing supper. In my attempt to get out of his way, I bumped into him. He grabbed me and slung me into the wall, grabbed me by the hair and started yelling at me. He slapped me across the mouth and told me to shut up."

Grace paused, took a deep breath, and bit her lip. Finally she went on.

"Suddenly he let me go and slumped to the floor. As he fell forward, I could see a butcher knife sticking from his back."

"What happened after that is a blur. My mother called 911 and when the medical people got there, they called the police, or somebody did, anyway the police came."

"My father died that night and my mother was charged with murder. My grandmother, my mother's mother, came and got me and my sister when they took Mother away."

"Surely they couldn't convict your mother of murder under those circumstances."

"You obviously have never run into the kind of justice the good old boy system turns out. My grandmother lived in a town about a hundred miles away and I was too young to attend any of the trial anyway. Later on, I thought my testimony might have helped her, but the trial was swift, the justice absent, and the next thing we knew Mother had been sent to the state prison for twenty years."

Lee pressed Grace to his chest as she softly sobbed. "How awful for you. But Grace, I'm here for you now."

"Let me finish since I've started my story."

"Anyway, my younger sister and I lived with my grandmother after that. I finished high school and was fortunate enough to get a scholarship for my college degree. When my grandmother died, she left me enough money to complete some post graduate work, and now here I am with the awful tragedy still haunting me."

"Couldn't your mother's case be re-opened? She doesn't deserve that kind of punishment. Did she plead self defense at her trial?"

"The prosecutor said it wasn't self defense because my father wasn't attacking her. After all the years he beat her up, that one time, she was showing motherly instinct and protecting me, her child, and not defending herself."

"How did Billy Bob find this out?"

"I have no idea, but it is causing me the loss of sleep and affecting my work, and certainly affecting my relationship with you."

"And will you go to see your mother during the Christmas holidays?"

"I hadn't planned to, but now I think I will. My sister probably won't go see her. She rarely does. I'll plan to be there after Christmas for the short visit that's allowed."

"I'll go with you." Lee offered.

"Wouldn't that look just great? With Billy Bob's edict about proper conduct for faculty members, we couldn't possibly get on an airplane here without someone finding that out, too."

They sat quietly for awhile. Then Lee broke the silence.

"Go with me to my home town, Chattanooga, Tennessee. We can spend Christmas day with my folks, and then fly out of there to Kansas. Nobody will know then."

Grace thought awhile. "That might work," she said. "I do want you to go with me. You are very important to me, do you understand that?"

"More than you know. Grace, I'd intended to ask you to marry me when we went to see my folks for the holidays. I wanted to introduce you as my fiancé. Instead, I'll just ask you now. Grace, will you marry me?"

CHAPTER SIX

It was still dark when Lee arrived in front of Grace's house to pick her up for the trip to his parents' home in Chattanooga. He had thought of little else since the night he had asked Grace to marry him. She hadn't said yes, but then she hadn't said no either. She had only looked at Lee and smiled and said, "Lee Castleberry, you are a dear man."

"I had hoped for more of an answer than that," Lee said.

"In time, in time." Grace put her arms about Lee's neck and kissed him fiercely. Of course he responded and that lead to the rest of the night.

Lee thought the time before the holidays began would never pass, but it had, and now he was picking up the love of his life to take to meet his parents. For the next two weeks, they would not have to deal with St. Bonnie's or anything or anybody affiliated with the school.

As they drove north along the interstate, Lee wanted to bring up getting married while they were in Tennessee, but he couldn't find the right opening to start that conversation.

His folks seemed delighted to see him and to meet Grace, who was put in Lee's old bedroom, while he was delegated to the day bed on the sleeping porch in the back of the house. His brother, who was to arrive Christmas Eve, was to share that space with Lee.

There was still no occasion for Lee to bring up marriage with Grace so he suggested they go shopping Christmas Eve. As they drove toward the malls, Lee said, "The truth is, I haven't bought your Christmas present yet, but I wanted you to be with me when I got it."

Grace studied Lee and said, "Okay."

Lee was impatient as they wandered through several department stores. "It's getting late," he said, "Let's get out of here and go select your present."

Lee steered Grace out of Belk's and down the walkway to Kay's Jewelry Store.

They entered the jewelry store and approached a clerk who was standing behind the counter looking as if he wanted to close up and go home. Lee couldn't blame him. It was Christmas Eve and already one o'clock in the afternoon.

"May I help you?" The clerk managed a small smile.

"We'd like to look at engagement rings," Lee said at once.

Grace looked at him and said, "Just a minute here. We haven't agreed to anything."

Sensing a good sale before closing and an upcoming holiday, the clerk perked up.

"We have some beautiful rings that will make you happy and enrich your life together. Let me show you some." He moved to the back of the counter again and took a key and unlocked the glass counter.

"Here's a gorgeous engagement ring, a full carat, set in beautiful yellow gold." He held up the ring.

Grace glared at Lee. "We need to speak privately about this."

The clerk put the ring back in the display counter and moved away. "I'll give you a few minutes alone," he said, "Then I'll be back to help you with your decision."

When the clerk had gone beyond earshot, Grace turned to Lee. "Have you lost your mind? We can't get married yet, not at this time."

"Why not? There's a beautiful little Episcopal church not far from here. We can't go back to St. Bonaventure and face the scandal of a holiday spent off together without the benefit of clergy. We'll be fired for sure when that word gets out. This is a simple way to stop any gossip that may await our return. Besides," Lee looked at Grace with great seriousness. "Besides, Grace, in the short time we've known each other, it cannot have escaped your notice that I have grown fond of you, nay, more than fond. Can this be love?"

"Come off your Rhett Butler speech," Grace said, but she did smile as she said it. "This isn't *Gone with the Wind*."

"We'll be gone with the wind if we go back unmarried. Come on, Grace, this is the best of all worlds. I love you. I want to spend the rest of my life with you. So why shouldn't we get married now while it will not only make us a happy couple, but solve so many other dilemmas."

"I certainly hadn't planned to be married at this particular time, but if you are willing to take me with all my excess baggage; you're willing to go with me to visit my mother in prison, that says a lot. Why not? You're smart and sweet and a terrific lover. I think it would be wonderful to be married." Grace motioned to the clerk who came running back.

"I don't know what you're planning to pay for these rings with," she whispered to Lee.

"There's always plastic," Lee smiled.

They spent forty-five minutes examining diamond engagement rings, and finally picked one that was a half carat. When the clerk suggested matching wedding bands, Grace said no that they could get them later. Things were going so well Lee decided not to push that point right now.

Lee got out his credit card and rolled his eyes to the ceiling when he saw the total amount for the ring. But the afternoon was turning out far better than he ever anticipated so he cheerfully signed for the purchase.

"Allow me," Lee said and took the diamond ring and slipped it on Grace's hand.

"How romantic can we get? Will you marry me, Grace?"

The clerk hid his laugh behind his hand. "Thank you very much for your business," he said. "I hope you'll have a very happy life together. And a Merry Christmas."

Lee and Grace skipped out of the store. "This calls for a celebration," Lee said. "Let's get a bottle of champagne and take it home and tell my folks. My mother is going to be so happy."

"Probably so, but I don't think she's going to let me move out of the guest room, or let you move in for that matter, just because we bring home a new ring and a bottle of champagne."

"It will be a Merry Christmas for everyone anyway," Lee assured her.

And it was indeed a Merry Christmas day. They had a scrumptious meal of turkey, cornbread dressing, lots of side dishes and ended with fruit ambrosia made with fresh oranges and coconut.

Things had grown quiet and the fire was dying down in the grate. Everyone else seemed to be somewhere else and only Lee and Grace sat on the sofa.

"We still have to go to Kansas, remember?" Grace said.

"Yes, and we still have to get married. I checked with my

dad and the courthouse is going to be open tomorrow so we can get the license. He said there's a justice of the peace in the court house who can perform the ceremony."

"I'd hoped for something a little more meaningful than that," Grace said.

"We can always check with the little church," Lee said at once. "You're not changing your mind, are you? You aren't going to back out?"

"No, I won't back out. And I suppose tomorrow is as good a day as any. We need to hurry up because we leave the next day for Kansas and there won't be time when we get back."

"I wish we could drive to Kansas and then go straight back home, but with winter weather a possibility and the time it would take to drive, we're better off flying out there and back like we planned in the first place. We'll have one more day here and can take our time driving back to St. Bonaventure."

Grace gave no further argument, and bright and early the afternoon after Christmas, Grace Garland and Lee Castleberry were married by the rector at the Church of the Holy Innocents. Lee's father served as best man and Grace's sister Karen, who had breezed in late Christmas Day was maid of honor although she left immediately after the short ceremony, wishing them the best, but stating she had a big project due before the end of the year and that there was no way she could accompany them to see their mother in Kansas.

And so Mr. and Mrs. Castleberry boarded a flight the next day and flew to Kansas.

Lee was not prepared for the prison experience. The building was old and dark and the day had turned overcast as well adding to the gloom. It took forever, he thought, to get through the red tape so that they could see Grace's mother.

Lee didn't comment but as the procedure was unfolding, he couldn't help but note it was much easier now that they were married. He could only imagine the complications had they arrived as daughter of the prisoner and her boyfriend.

Finally they were led to a plain room with gray painted walls. Three chairs were placed at a table. Lee and Grace took two of them. Presently, a guard brought Grace's mother into the room and went to stand by the door.

Lee could see where Grace got her beauty. Her mother had the same facial shape and coloring, same eyes, nose and mouth. Though she looked haggard and tired, she was still a beautiful woman, Lee thought.

"Mother, how are you?" Grace took both her mother's hands in hers. "You look well. Are they treating you all right?"

"As well as could be expected," Grace's mother said. "Who is this you've brought with you? I thought your sister Karen was coming?"

"Mother," Grace turned to Lee. "Karen couldn't make it today, but I'd like to introduce my husband, Lee Castleberry."

Grace's mother studied Lee carefully. "I hope you're a good man," she said. "Grace deserves a good man in her life. You had better treat her right. If you don't I'll find a way to get out of here and make you pay."

Lee felt a chill go down his spine. "Mrs. Garland, I think I'm the luckiest man alive to have Grace for my wife. I give you my solemn promise that I will hold her in the greatest respect and love her dearly the rest of her life."

"That's good to hear." She turned to Grace. "Congratulations, my dear, I hope you have better luck in your marriage than I had in mine."

They chatted awhile longer, mostly Grace and her mother, with Lee sitting with his hands in his lap. Then the guard looked at his watch and said it was time for the visit to be over.

Grace hugged her mother for a long time. "Oh Mother," she said, "If there was only something I could do to get you out of here."

"Time's up," the guard said.

Lee and Grace walked silently back to the entrance of the prison and went out the front door into the gloom of twilight.

Lee was thinking of the time and money they had spent to get here for this short visit. But, if Grace was happy, he was pleased and had no regrets.

"There's got to be something we can do," Lee said. "I will not stop till I find it. We have to get your mother out of this awful place."

CHAPTER SEVEN

After Lee and Grace had arrived on the flight from Kansas, they went to bed early—together in the guest room—without so much as a nod from Lee's parents. They were up early the next morning for the long and tiresome drive back home.

The trip took nearly all day. About half way, Lee said, "I really wish we'd bought that matching pair of wedding rings."

"Doesn't matter. We're still married," Grace said. She looked out the window at the passing scene.

"I'll get you a wedding band the very next payday."

"You've already spent enough on this engagement ring."

"I wish it could have been a carat," Lee looked at the Interstate sign they were passing marking the mileage to the next exit. "Do you want to stop and get something to eat?"

"No, if it's all the same to you, I'd rather keep going and get home as soon as possible. I'll drive if you're tired."

They did stop for gas and to switch drivers and finally arrived on the outskirts of town shortly after dark. The winter night was cold and dreary and not much traffic was on the streets.

"Why don't we go to my place to spend the night?" Grace spoke.

"Fine with me."

As they unpacked the car, Lee picked up several newspapers which had accumulated in the yard.

"Didn't you stop the paper?"

"Yes," Grace said, "But they never get it right."

They settled into the apartment and Grace went into the kitchen. "There's nothing here to eat but some soup. Do you want to go to the grocery and pick up something?"

"Soup sounds good to me. I don't want to drive another block." Lee sat down and unfolded one of the newspapers. Some were yellow from exposure.

He flipped through the front sections and turned to the local news.

"Oh, my God!" Lee gasped.

"What is it?" Grace rushed to his side.

"Look at this headline. It says Ben Baker was killed in an automobile accident while we were gone."

"Oh, no, not Ben. He was such a great kid. How did it happen?"

"A bunch of the fellows were out during the holidays. Driving home from a Christmas party, the car was apparently traveling at a high rate of speed and spun off the road into a clump of trees. Ben was killed outright and two of the other four boys were taken to local hospitals in serious and critical condition."

"That's just awful." Grace sat on the sofa and sighed. "We must go visit his parents. Does it say when the funeral will be held?

Lee searched through several more pages for the obituary page.

"It's already been held, three days after Christmas. This is an old paper."

"Things won't be the same at school Monday. Poor Ben. I'll have to get there early."

Grace wiped her eyes. Slowly she got up and went to the stove to check the soup.

"I'll always remember the last time I saw Ben," Lee said. "Remember he was jogging down the street right in front of this house when we left for Chattanooga. No one else saw us leave together, but we knew Ben would never say anything. What a way to say goodbye to such a remarkable young man. Gosh, I'll miss him."

Grace came in bringing a tray with two bowls of soup.
"Lee, in light of this tragedy, I think it might be a good thing if we didn't announce our marriage until things settle down about Ben."

"You mean keep it a secret?"

"Yes, no-- not that. But the student body will be in shock and very upset over Ben's death. We can't push a happy occasion like our wedding into the scene right now. Let's let them grieve for the time being."

"If you say so," Lee said. He didn't like the idea; but he was tired from the long drive, and too shaken by the death of one of his favorite students to argue. Who would keep the stats now he thought? How awful to raise a son to a senior in high school and then lose him during Christmas of all seasons. Lee wondered more about the accident. He wondered if anyone had been drinking. Ever faithful Ben, who would never tell on any of his buddies, would have kept his mouth shut even if it cost him his life, which it very well may have.

Grace was right. There was a pall over the student body on the Monday when Christmas holidays ended and school reopened. A special memorial chapel was held for Ben. There was much weeping and a lot of hugging. The rector from St. Bonaventure's church spoke, Billy Bob as headmaster had some words, several of the students had remarks and the school chorus sang "*Amazing Grace*" and "*Nearer My God to Thee.*"

It was rather a strange thing that they sang "Amazing Grace" because the students often sang that to Grace though she didn't really like that or approve of it. A chill ran through Lee's mind as he realized they were singing that hymn as a farewell to Ben. He never wanted to hear it again, never wanted to associate it with his Grace whom he wanted to keep forever, his adored wife he couldn't even acknowledge at the moment.

As usual Grace was right and this was not the time to announce their marriage. The memorial ended with a member of the band playing taps. Everyone in the church crying, even the big football linemen.

As they came out, Grace pulled Lee over and said, "Mr. Castleberry, have you met Ben's parents?"

"No," Lee said. "And I am so sorry for the circumstances which cause us to meet at this time. I thought a lot of Ben. He and I got to know each other well in my office where, as you doubtless know, he kept all the sports stats on his computer. By the way, his computer is still in my office. You'll want to come pick it up, I imagine."

Ben's father shook Lee's hand and held it a bit longer. "No, Mr. Castleberry. We want you to have Ben's laptop. He thought so much of you. He was so pleased you let him share your office and do the stats. And, he told us you sometimes used the laptop to write press releases. Ben would want you to have the computer. We want you to have it."

"I don't know what to say," Lee stammered. "Thank you. It will mean a great deal to me to have something that was Ben's. I'll always think of him when I use it."

"It will be comforting to know something Ben loved is still

being used at St. Bonaventure by someone he admired so highly," Mrs. Baker said, as she buried her face in a handkerchief and turned away.

Things slowly began to get back to normal at the school by the end of the week, but the mid-winter doldrums had settled in. Students were lethargic; faculty didn't seem to have much enthusiasm. The days dragged.

Billy Bob called a faculty meeting and for once, didn't begin with "I know you're wondering why I called you here today."

"This will be a short meeting," he said. "We appreciate your help in trying to get the student body through this tragic period. But, we have to get on with our lives and help them get on with theirs."

"The big state indoor track meet is being held in Montgomery the end of February. St. Bonnie needs to be represented in that event. Grace, I want you to get some girls together and coach and take them to the meet. Lee, you'll do the same for the boys."

"There's not much time to prepare," Grace noted.

"I know you'll think of something," Billy Bob said. "And Lee can always handle anything I give him to do. For the group, that's all. Grace, will you and Lee stay a little longer please?"

Billy Bob looked at Grace's hand and spotted the diamond ring. "Well, Well, Grace," he said, "Is that a Christmas present or an engagement ring?" He laughed. Then he gave them a nervous smile.

Grace cut her eyes to Lee and then turned to Billy Bob. "Let's just say it's a Christmas present."

"Really? And where did you spend the holidays?" Billy Bob raised one eyebrow.

Grace looked at Lee again and remained silent. At that moment, the class bell rang and Grace dashed out the door saying she had a class and had to get her roll book from her office and hurry to her class room."

"Does she seem to be acting strange to you?" Billy Bob asked Lee.

"No, she seems to be acting perfectly normal to me," Lee said, thinking to himself that Grace had certainly been saved by the bell. "Now if you'll excuse me, too, I have a lot to do if we're going to take a track team to the State Indoor Meet in such a short time."

Lee called a meeting of the football team and asked for

volunteers to run track. A handful of the young men offered, and with Lee, they began to determine who would participate in which event. Lee had kept the time sheet for the football tryouts and was able to select some sprinters from that group. He picked several of the big defense players for the shot put, and one of the lanky receivers told Lee he had done high jump in the City Recreation Department program the preceding year. No one challenged him for that event.

Lee went to Grace's apartment that night. He would always think of it as her apartment. His was not as large. They needed to find a place of their own. They needed to stop pretending they weren't married and settle down.

Lee got home before Grace, who came in soon thereafter. "How'd your girls track team go?" Lee asked.

"I was surprised by a large turnout. Several of the girls participated in the City Recreational program last summer. They are already in pretty good shape and know what to expect. One of them is especially good at the mile run."

"That's good. I've got a boy who did City Rec, too, and we have some pretty good runners on the football team who agreed to run the sprints. I don't know what to do about the distance runners."

"If we practice the two teams together, that should help. Also, I think they would enjoy each other's company and make that a morale booster."

"We'll set it up tomorrow then," Lee said. "Grace, when do you want to tell Billy Bob about us, about our marriage? You evaded him nicely after the faculty meeting today, but he's no fool. He will figure out something pretty quick. Either he's going to know we are living together and make a big scene about that, or we'll have to confess we are Mr. and Mrs."

"I know you're right, Lee," Grace said, "But I can't deal with it right now... Maybe after we get back from the track meet, we can get him aside and tell him."

"I don't understand why we have to keep it secret."

"I don't have a wedding ring," Grace said and smiled.

"You have a piece of paper that says you are married, and you have a husband who adores you," Lee said. "Tomorrow I'll see that you have a wedding ring, the band of gold."

"You're right," Grace said. "What do you want for supper?"

"Nothing yet. I'd like an appetizer first," and Lee pulled Grace into the bedroom.

Lee kept his promise and the next afternoon, he hurried to the local jewelry shop. Fortunately, he did not have a class the last period which gave him time to go and buy the ring and get back to school in time for the new track team joint practice.

Grace already had the girls and boys stretching. As she had predicted, the boys were delighted to be practicing with the girls. This allowed them to show off their athletic skills. Being young masculine creatures, they were, of course, stronger and faster than the girls, but that was of no consequence since they did not have to compete against each other. Camaraderie developed almost at once with each group lending encouragement to the other group and cheering them on.

As it grew dark, the practice ended. Lee and Grace sent the teams on their way checked the field for any items which had been left.

A moon was rising in the east and Lee caught Grace by the arm and pulled her back to him. He took the gold wedding band from his pocket and slipped it on to Grace's finger. "Now you're really Mrs. Lee Castleberry," he said.

CHAPTER EIGHT

Lee

How much longer do we have to keep up this pretence? Grace and I are legally married, I love her very much; I am happy she is my wife. Why can't we tell the world? Why do we have to sneak around here with Billy Bob, the faculty, and the board of trustees?

I want us to be together and face the whole world. We need to be living together in peace, not stressed out like this.

I don't like the attitude Billy Bob is taking. He seems to be against everything I try to do. And heaven knows, I'm doing a whole lot more than I ever agreed to do. I'm still not satisfied to be here in this school situation, and I don't think I ever will be. I don't want to be a school teacher, but I don't know what to do about it. I do know I want to be where Grace is, and if it weren't for St. Bonnie's, I never would have met her.

I wish she'd open up more with me and tell me what she's thinking. The situation would be much better here if she'd let us make our marriage announcement. I just don't understand why she wants to wait.

She was really upset at the State Indoor Track Meet. When I came back from lunch with the boys and found her eyeball to eyeball with Sonny Brown, the head of the State High School Athletic Association, I could tell she was really mad. They call him Sweet Ole Brownie, or usually just those initials.

He really is a son of a bitch and way out of date with his thinking toward women, but I doubt he's met anyone as forceful as Grace in her stand. She told me later he refused to let our best female runner participate in the relay because she had run the mile in the morning and it wasn't healthy for a female to run more than a mile in one day. He pointed out the rules for girls, which are much more restricted than those for the boys.

Grace lit into him and told him that his statement was contrary to all scientific and medical data. His reply was that **he** didn't think it was healthy, therefore the girls wouldn't run since he said they wouldn't. It cost us the championship, no doubt about that. We only had ten girls and his edict wiped out both the long and short relays as well as the half mile, all of which we would have probably won.

Grace fumed all the way home, and then when Billy Bob called her in Monday morning and told her Sweet Ole Brownie had called and demanded Grace be fired for being a "troublemaker," her rage was felt all over the building.

"The nerve of that ignorant chauvinist pig, calling Billy Bob and telling him to fire me," Grace said to me Monday night. "No doubt Billy Bob is right though," she went on. "If this was a public school, I'd be gone. It's wrong for one man to have so much power in a state educational situation. That's the way he controls football, though I don't think any young ladies have tried to play football yet. They will though, in time they will, they'll want to play football, too. The state simply has to get rid of those antique rules which are so different for boys and girls."

I wonder if Grace can make that happen. I guess I'll just have to play things by ear. But I still want everyone to know we're married.

Grace

Well, I've written this letter to the government department HEW filing a complaint for discrimination against girls in sports in this state. That's what Title IX is all about—fairness in the athletic teams for both sexes. I don't plan to tell Lee until I get this letter in the mail. Then I'll show Lee a copy of it. Otherwise, he might try to get me to change it, or not send it at all. He'll support me though, I know that.

And, we are going to have to let the world know about our marriage soon. It isn't fair to Lee. It isn't fair to me either for that matter. I guess I don't know why I'm hesitating. I'm sure Billy Bob isn't going to like it, but then it isn't his life. Lee is a wonderful man, and I love him and think we will have a long happy life together. I certainly wouldn't have gone into a marriage unless I felt that way. But it was a bit sudden. I never dreamed when we left here for Christmas vacation that I'd come back a married woman.

Billy Bob isn't treating Lee very well these days. I really wonder what his reaction is going to be to our wedding news. And how dare Sweet Ole Brownie tell Billy Bob to fire me? St.

Bonaventure of all schools should be promoting the equality of women and girls. The current rules went out of date with World War One. The Civil Rights Act of 1973 assures an equal playing field for both men and women. Otherwise, the institutions discriminating against women stand to lose their federal money. But then St. Bonnie doesn't get any federal money. Since we operate under a church name, we certainly should push for women's rights regardless. But will Billy Bob feel that way? Will the board of trustees see it in that light? Nothing to do but post this letter and see what happens. If Sonny Brown gets a mandate from the federal government, he will have no alternative but to change the state athletic rules and make them equal.

I better get out of here and mail this letter before anything else happens.

Billy Bob

What's with Lee and Grace? They are acting so differently since the Christmas holidays. How could Grace have made such a scene in Montgomery when she knows how hard we're working to get a good reputation in the city and the state for being a school of excellence? And then the chairman of the board tells me that the headmaster should have a wife–that it would just "look better". I'm getting to that. I've picked Grace for that role, and now she has to go do something like this and get the wrong kind of attention.

But again, if it gets out we aren't pushing all our teams, both boys and girls, then our reputation won't be enhanced any. Grace is right. The rules stink when they are so different for girls. And it would have been nice to win the state track meet which we probably would have if all our girls been allowed to participate in all their events.

Sonny Brown isn't concerned with anything but football anyway. Why is he interfering with girls track? Because he's power mad, of course. He isn't content to dictate football policy. He had to get involved in track, girls track at that. But he probably has met his match in Grace. She doesn't sit still for any idea she disagrees with especially when she feels as strongly as she does about women's rights. I guess I'd better promote my courtship with Grace with more vigor. I think she's still mad about Thanksgiving dinner when

I left her to go to the board chairman's house. She has to understand the political necessities of being headmaster.

I answer to the board, but Sonny Brown isn't going to dictate to me. I didn't tell him I'd fire Grace. That would be very ill advised. First of all, I couldn't replace her as academic dean, and we couldn't operate St. Bonnie without her. And second, I need to build my relationship with Grace and make her my wife as soon as possible.

I told Sweet Ole Brownie I'd check into the situation. It won't be a factor again for awhile. I'll just let the whole thing ride. I'll ask Grace to dinner this week end.

But the way Lee and Grace are acting, it's almost as if they are in a relationship. That fouls up my plan, and we can't have any romances at St. Bonnie except mine. I'll call them in again and emphasize the importance of presenting the very best character profiles to the rest of the world. Yes, I'll call them back in and go over that more emphatically. I have a feeling I need to woo Grace and get her as my wife as soon as possible.

* * *

"I'm sure you wonder why I called you here today," Billy Bob began at the next faculty meeting. "We have to be very aware of the gossip and scuttle butt that can come from out chatting in the faculty lounge and in the local grocery stores and village shops. Discussing school events and especially school personnel can be very destructive to our purpose and our goals in education.

"Therefore, I ask that you refrain from talking about any school situations, any student or any faculty member under any circumstances. That's all on the agenda today. Lee and Grace, can you stay a few more minutes please?"

What now? Lee thought. He kept the same seat he had been in for the regular faculty meeting. Grace, however, moved over and sat next to him.

"I'm sorry I have to say this," Billy Bob started, "But you two are causing a lot of the gossip circulating. You are together entirely too much, more than two faculty members normally would be together. I will have to ask you to stop sitting together at the lunch room and stop visiting in each other's offices. Even though I ask the faculty not to talk about such things, it is fairly obvious that you two have a lot of togetherness. It just has to stop, do you understand?"

Grace leaned over and whispered something to Lee. He nodded and said something back to her.

"Now that's just exactly what I'm talking about," Billy Bob snapped.

"You or me?" Grace said to Lee.

"I'll do it. It's my place don't you think?"

"Billy Bob," Lee began. "There's something Grace and I have to tell you."

"I hope it's that you will correct your conduct around school."

"Billy Bob, Lee and I were married the day after Christmas," Grace blurted out.

"You were what?" He sat down.

"We were married in Chattanooga the day after Christmas," Lee stated.

"Well, why didn't you tell me before?" The color had drained from Billy Bob's face and he was positively pale.

"We're telling you now." Lee and Grace spoke together.

"This is quite a shock to me," Billy Bob said. "I have to think about what to do about this. I don't understand why you kept this secret."

"The proper time and place hasn't presented itself until now," Lee continued.

"Things were hectic when the Christmas holidays ended. Ben Baker's death was a shock to everyone and we didn't want to take any dignity from that sad event. We weren't keeping it secret so much as we were waiting for the proper time and place. Now you've asked so we're telling you."

"I don't know what we'll do about this?" Billy Bob blew out his breath.

"There's nothing for you to do." Lee said. "It isn't illegal to marry. We can tell the faculty individually or have a big meeting and tell them, whatever you want to do."

"We aren't set up at St. Bonnie to have married faculty in the same department or at least in the same high school division. We can be accused of nepotism."

Grace spoke up. "When we were both single and had never

met when school started, how in the world we can be accused of nepotism? St. Bonnie has such a pleasant atmosphere and such fine people teaching at the institution, we found we had a lot in common and we wanted to get married. It's that simple."

Billy Bob stood up again. "But I thought," he started. "I'll have to think about it. Go on back to your classes or your offices. This is just a real shock to me. I'll have to think more about what to do."

Lee took Grace by the hand and led her out before anything else could be said. In the hallway Lee said, "I never expected him to react that way."

"He did behave strangely," Grace said. "All the talk and saying he didn't know what to do. I think he's under a lot of pressure and not behaving rationally."

"Let's beat him to the punch and tell some people now," Lee said. "Let's go in the faculty lounge and yell to the high heavens that we're married."

"Let's think more about moving in together. That's more important than irritating Billy Bob even further." Grace said.

"Whatever you say, you're right of course." Lee said. He left Grace at her office door and went on to the gym to his little cubby-hole office under the bleachers. For the first time since the day after Christmas, he felt like a really married man. And he liked the feeling.

Lee was therefore surprised the next day in the faculty lounge when one of the teachers looked up from her coffee cup and said, "Have you heard the latest?"

"No, what is the latest?" Lee asked.

"We're getting a new headmaster," she said.

"You mean Billy Bob is leaving?"

"We don't know. He may be assistant headmaster. But someone new is coming from outside. Nobody seems to know why or when."

"That's certainly interesting news," Lee said. He went over to the coffee urn and poured himself a cup of coffee.

"Where did you hear this?" He sat down at the table with the teacher.

"Oh, everybody knows it," she said. "I heard it last Friday in the Food World from a parent who is married to someone on the board of trustees."

"Well, if everybody knows that must make it so, huh?"

"Certainly. Why else would everybody be talking about it?"

"I guess they don't have much else to talk about," Lee said. He picked up the newspaper which was always in the faculty lounge. The other teacher picked up her coffee cup and left.

That must be why Billy Bob gave his little speech about not gossiping, Lee thought. He couldn't wait to talk to Grace about this little item. He wondered who the new man might be. He hoped he would be easier to get along with than Billy Bob had been lately. But whatever, Lee thought; he was stuck here until the end of the school year. Then maybe he and Grace could go somewhere else and get a new start.

CHAPTER NINE

The gossip in the teachers' lounge grew more frequent in spite of Billy Bob's urging and warning against it. Parents stopped teachers in the grocery store and asked if the rumors of the school getting a new headmaster were true. The teachers mumbled and said they didn't know, that no announcement had been made, that we'd have to wait and see. But the talk went on.

Was a new headmaster coming, and if so who would it be? What would happen to Billy Bob? Would he be assistant headmaster? Why was there a need to have a new head or assistant at this time? It was a strange time of year to make such changes. Wasn't everything running smoothly?

Lee and Grace tried to ignore the talk as best they could. After considering their options, they moved into Grace's apartment. Her place was closer to the school, and she had more room and a better equipped kitchen. Lee moved some of his belongings; but his lease had some time to go so they used his apartment for storage of things they wanted to keep and gave the rest to the Water Front Mission Society who sent a truck for the items.

The rest of the faculty congratulated the newly married couple and threw a spontaneous party for them in the teachers' lounge after school one day. A designated faculty member presented them with a sizable check. "We thought you probably had accumulated enough pots and pots between the two of you, so we took a collection of money to let you get what you want for a wedding present."

In the meantime, no announcement came from the board of trustees regarding any administrative changes, and everyone began to think it was just a rumor, and nothing more.

Billy Bob went around with a frown on his face most of the time. He carried a pocket tape recorder and spoke into it frequently, making notes and comments which he later gave to his secretary to translate into letters or directives to the faculty.

He sent Lee a memo stating that any scheduling for any team Lee was coaching was to be approved by him, Billy Bob, before any contracts were signed. Lee thought about going to Billy

Bob to discuss this. Lee felt he was not being trusted to make decisions. He also thought Billy Bob had enough to do without micro managing the athletic schedules. Lee resented the new controls which were being placed on his job. Billy Bob just didn't seem like the same person he had known in college. Did being head of a growing school cause this much stress? In the old days Lee could have talked to Billy Bob about anything. Not now. Things just weren't the same. Lee felt he had no latitude to carry on his job or work independently. He felt his academic freedom was being threatened though he was only teaching two actual classes. This was, all in all, just not a good situation. If Billy Bob didn't think Lee was doing a good job, why couldn't he just tell him and not put all these barriers in his path?

It didn't stop with Lee. Grace came home and told Lee that Billy Bob was asking that she not send any reports she wrote or made for the Southern Association without his approval and editing if necessary.

Both Lee and Grace felt very frustrated.

"He's mad because we're married," Grace said

"No, he's jealous because we're married," Lee added. "His tough luck." He put his arm around Grace.

They discussed the situation every night and decided to send out some feelers for new positions. Neither of them wanted to go into the public schools and the field of independent educators was limited in the town. Lee wanted out of the educational field entirely, but he didn't want to jeopardize Grace's chances at any new position. They considered that maybe it was better for Lee to leave St. Bonnie's and for Grace to stay. Whatever, the atmosphere at St. Bonnie was very stormy and the couple did not want to plan a career in that kind of environment. What should they do? They decided that there wasn't much they could do for the remainder of the school term. They finally agreed talking about it only made things worse and mutually agreed to drop the subject until something happened at St. Bonnie to make it feasible to bring it up again.

The question was soon solved by the arrival of Ted Walker who was announced as the new headmaster. There was a big picture of him in the newspaper and a write up done by one of the trustees. Lee bristled at the poor public relations action in the way this was handled. He resented the fact that he held the title of public relations director and was not advised, consulted, or asked to write an announcement of this importance. The faculty was not told in advance, and they were furious when they all read it in the local newspaper.

"The least they could have done was tell us in advance," one said.

"Yes, it's embarrassing to have a parent stop you in the grocery store and ask how we like the new headmaster when none of the faculty even knew we had a new head," said another.

So resentment boiled on all sides. Many took Billy Bob's side and said he'd got a raw deal, that he was doing a good job and there was no need to replace him. Others said he had become overbearing with his edicts and micro managing.

Lee sympathized with Billy Bob even though he had been displeased with the manner in which Billy Bob had approached his work of late. His old friend didn't deserve this kind of thing, Lee thought. Billy Bob had even appointed many of the board members earlier when the school was struggling. Then at least enough of them to make a majority had turned their allegiance against Billy Bob and lowered his position to assistant headmaster.

Lee wondered if they had talked to Billy Bob about it, or had questioned him about things they didn't like. Lee later found out Billy Bob read it in the paper himself. Is that a way to run a school? Lee thought.

While Lee was wondering what kind of boss Ted Walker would be, he was called into the office of the new man.

"I'm trying to get around and meet everyone," he said, "and see what each person is doing and how they are operating their department or class. But that takes time. So for the time being, I'm telling everyone to carry on as before. We won't make any drastic changes for awhile. However, we need to raise some money quickly. I want you to set up a charity golf tournament. You know the format."

"I'm not much of a golfer," Lee protested. "I'm not sure what you have in mind."

"Oh, it's easy. Get a few celebrities to be guests, set up a four-man best ball play and have a big day of it. We need to charge a sizable entry fee per team, not charge the famous folks of course, but if we can get a hundred or so signed up, we'll have a good sum in the till for the budget. Get started on it right away, will you, Lee?"

Lee got up to leave. "One more thing," Ted said. "We'll need attractions to draw the families to the event. I'm appointing your wife Grace to be in charge of food booths, pony rides for the children, games, hot dogs, you know."

"Have you given any thought as to which course we are to play on?" Lee asked.

"I'm new around here, but we want to get the best golf course in town, or in the area. Isn't there one of those Robert Trent Jones courses near here?" Ted said.

"There are two," Lee said. "One is west of here with fifty four holes. The other is across the bay at the Grand Hotel; both of them are Robert Trent Jones courses."

"The Grand Hotel sound elegant. Get that one. And report to me each day on the progress."

Lee left Ted's office wondering what else could go wrong with this school year. Except for marrying Grace, he felt the whole term had been a dismal failure.

It was lunch time and Lee remembered he had lunch room duty—one more thing he despised. It interrupted his day and the noise gave him a frequent headache. He got to the lunch room and discovered he was sharing the duty with Billy Bob.

"How is it going, man?" Lee asked. He could think of nothing else to say.

"Great," Billy Bob answered, "Just like a fireplace, grate." He laughed at his own joke and slapped Lee on the shoulder.

"In the light of what's happened, you seem mighty chipper," Lee got a tray and started down the cafeteria line. Billy Bob followed.

"Might as well be optimistic," Billy Bob said. "There's nothing I can do about the recent events. The board of trustees has spoken. I thought about it a long time and decided they did me a favor. I'll have less stress, less to do, and I won't have to raise the money we need right now."

"I get to do that," Lee growled.

"What do you mean?" Billy Bob asked.

"Walker just appointed me to head a charity golf

tournament. You know I don't know anything about golf. How am I going to persuade one hundred people to pay mega bucks for a day of golf?"

Billy Bob laughed. "A day of golf always costs mega bucks," he said. "I'll help, I play a bit of golf and I know others who play, too. Where will this tournament be held?"

"Walker wants it at the Grand Hotel course."

"Oh boy," Billy Bob whistled. "That may not be so easy to come by. We will have to talk the facilities management into donating a whole day or at least part of a day because we can never afford the green fees. They'd eat up the hundred dollar entry fee in a heartbeat and we'd still be lacking. No, the course will have to be donated."

"You are not very encouraging." Lee put his tray on the nearest table. Billy Bob joined him and they both sat down.

"Well, if you want me to, I'll make a few phone calls. At least I can see what the lay of the land is." Billy Bob said.

"We have to start somewhere I guess so that will be helpful. If you can get us a golf course to play on, then I'll start some marketing and see if I can get the entries coming in. By the way we need a couple of celebrities to anchor the players. Got any good ideas there?"

Billy Bob took a bite of his sandwich and thought a minute. "Do you know that country song writer named Topp Hatter?"

"No, I don't think I do."

"Well he has a little girl in the second grade in the lower school. I'll bet he'll come and play golf and add some country tunes as well if we ask him right."

"Do you know him well enough to ask him?" Lee asked.

"Sure, old buddy, I'll call the Grand Hotel golf course shop and talk to the pro and I will give old Topp Hatter a call. Don't you worry about a thing. The cavalry is on the way."

The bell ending the lunch period rang and the two men went their separate ways. Lee was puzzled at the new behavior of Billy Bob. Why's he being so nice now? Lee thought. He's been on my back ever since I came to St. Bonnie and now he's being all nice and offering to help me with this golf tournament about which I know nothing. He's running hot and cold, but right now I'll take all the help I can get.

Since Billy Bob had offered, Lee decided there was nothing to do but to chalk it up to good luck. He took a blank piece of paper and began to sketch a flyer for the golf tournament, something that would catch the eye. He wondered if he had a budget to print some. He would need to write a press release, he thought, and also get the announcement in the church bulletin. Grace could help recruit some of the ladies from the school families. Grace must play some golf, he thought, as he remembered moving some golf clubs from her closet to the storage area when they were combining their belongings. He kept finding out more and more new things he didn't know about his wife.

Maybe this new headmaster would turn the tide in this school year. The year had been challenging so far and it had nowhere to go but up. He happily remembered one of the football players played golf. He had been pictured in the local sports section for a junior event back in the fall when Lee first came. In fact he missed football practice one day to go play golf. Lee was glad now he had cheerfully allowed the boy to do that. Maybe there were others he didn't know about. Maybe he could make playing in the golf tournament a must on the to-do list of the teen agers at St. Bonnie.

Just maybe this would be the thing that salvaged the year. Lee opened the laptop, thought of Ben, and wondered if he had ever played golf.

Lee sighed and began to type.

CHAPTER TEN

Billy Bob came through with his promises. He made arrangements with the Grand Hotel golf course for the tournament to be played there on a Saturday. The school could have one of the courses the whole day. Lee didn't ask how Billy Bob managed to do this. He wasn't sure he wanted to know. Billy Bob also called Topp Hatter who said he would be happy to come and play; and not only would he come, but he would get some of his country music friends to attend as well if they wanted them. They did. At least Lee did. The more the better, he thought

So now Lee had stars of sorts in the lineup. He took one of his news releases to town to the local paper one day and happened to meet Ben Baker's father. They exchanged pleasantries and Lee told him how much he was enjoying the laptop and that he thought of Ben every time he turned it on. Mr. Baker seemed pleased and re-emphasized how much they had wanted Lee to have Ben's laptop. He said Lee's friendship had meant so much to Ben this school year. Ben's father continued. "He was so happy at St. Bonaventure and you contributed to that."

Mr. Baker asked Lee what brought him to town and when Lee told him he was delivering a news release to the newspaper on the St. Bonnie upcoming golf tournament, Mr. Baker smiled again and told Lee that was great, and that he would like to help. He had some good suggestions...

Mr. Baker said not only would he himself sign up to play, but he would get some of his business associates to form some teams and enter. He also said he'd ask his nephew to come to the tournament. Baker's nephew happened to be Sammy Worth, a professional golfer of some note. Lee thought things were shaping up nicely and felt relieved.

The ever efficient Grace not only got the ladies organized to handle the food and other entertainment, but Grace herself said she would play. Grace was a pretty good golfer Lee found out later. And to make things even nicer, Grace talked several of the mothers into playing which was good because the new headmaster wanted this to be a coed event and that if the women played, it would create more interest and get more men entered in the tournament. It turned out he was right about that.

Lee would have signed up to play himself but he thought better of it when he realized he would have to coordinate everything on the day the golf was played.

Lee went to the Grand Hotel to talk with the pro and be sure everything was in order. By the time the appointed Saturday rolled around, they ended up with over one hundred players.

The chosen Saturday was a beautiful day, sunny and not a cloud in the sky with the temperature mild and a slight breeze blowing. Lee and Grace got to the links very early in the morning and set up the last minute necessities. All the golf carts were lined up with the names of the players on the front and the hole to which they should go for the shotgun start.

Things went splendidly well. The team with Mr. Baker and one of the high school boys plus two of the St. Bonnie fathers who were local merchants won the eighteen-hole event with a five under par score. Handicaps were figured in to determine the first place winners. They and the next three teams won prizes: donated golf equipment– golf bags, clubs, boxes of balls-- and coupons for free play at a local Robert Trent Jones golf course.

The ladies provided an excellent seafood lunch and a local ice cream company even donated the desert. Everyone seemed to enjoy Topp Hatter and the sounds of the country music rang through the lovely old live oak trees which surrounded the clubhouse.

After nearly everyone had gone home, Lee and Grace were checking about the premises to be sure all the personal belongings had been claimed and the area was reasonably clean of litter. Ted Walker approached them and pounded Lee on the back.

"Great job, Castleberry," he said. "This is a banner day for St. Bonnie. Not only have you raised a sizable sum for our budget so that we can build the new gym, but the public relations you have generated are terrific. This should put St. Bonnie on the map in even greater fashion than we imagined."

Lee's happiness over the success of the golf tournament was short lived. Monday morning he looked up from his desk and saw Ted Walker coming into his office.

"You are a little crowded in here, aren't you?" Ted asked.

"I've gotten used to it by now," Lee answered. "I probably would get lost in a bigger place."

"Well, you will have a bigger office when we get the new gym especially since through your efforts, we were able to raise so much money. In fact, you are so good at raising money that I am going to make you not only director of public relations but director of development. That's a disguised way of saying you are the chief fund raiser."

Lee sighed. "I appreciate the compliment, but I really don't know anything about fund raising. My training is in public relations."

"I'm told you said you didn't know anything about coaching football, too," Ted smiled. "But I'm also told you did an excellent job of putting together a team and scheduling enough games that we can get into the state high school athletic association. Don't sell yourself short, Castleberry. You are a good man to have at St. Bonnie and I intend to use your talents."

With that remark, Ted Walker left Lee's office.

It's nice to be appreciated for a change, Lee thought. He still didn't want to be at St. Bonnie's next year, but now he realized he had to consider Grace's feelings on the matter. She had a nice title, one she had wanted and worked for as dean of academic affairs. And she was good at it. He might have to put up with another year of being here, more than just another year, if Grace was happy. Because, Lee somehow knew that if Grace wasn't happy, then he wouldn't be happy.

He would consider the advantages. Billy Bob seemed to be his old self again and Ted Walker was certainly complimentary of what Lee was doing and had done for St. Bonnie.

And they would have a new gym next year, but Lee realized he could not go on being football coach, track coach, golf tournament organizer, public relations director, and now development director. Some of those titles and those jobs had to be farmed out to someone else. Maybe Ted would have contracts for the coming school year. Lee felt he could suggest that to Ted and made up his mind that he would do that as soon as the opportunity presented itself.

As it so happened, Lee got the opportunity the next day when Ted called him in to review the final report of the golf tournament. All the bills had been paid and they had made a little more profit than had been anticipated.

"I have a suggestion for next year," Lee began. "We've never operated with contracts at St. Bonnie and I think it is time we get some things in writing."

"No contracts? I never heard of such a thing. But then I didn't ask either." Ted seemed shocked.

"It would be better all around for the school and for the faculty and other workers," Lee continued. "And I expect if anyone ever gets audited by the Internal Revenue Service, it would be extremely important to have a contract stating an amount of payment for services rendered."

"You're absolutely right," Ted said. "I'll get Benny Lawyer who is on the board of trustees to prepare a blank contract leaving space for the names of the individuals, the job descriptions, and the stated salary. I can't believe St. Bonnie has been operating without contracts."

Near the end of the school year, each faculty member was called into the headmaster's office to discuss jobs and contracts for the following year. Most faculty members didn't seem to think this was unusual. Some were not called in, however, which was a soft pedal manner of issuing a pink slip. Naturally this caused gossip in the faculty lounge and among the groups who gathered at the local tea shop and the aisles of the grocery stores.

Lee was wondering what he and Grace would be doing for the summer vacation when a final faculty meeting was held before the dismissal for the summer holiday.

"Lee," said Ted. "I want St. Bonnie to have a yearbook. There is a work shop at the State University this summer. You should go to that workshop. The school will pay your expenses, and so you won't be lonely, there is a seminar at the same time for the deans of academic affairs, so Grace, you can plan to go with Lee and take advantage of all this and make it a vacation learning experience."

That night as they sat after eating their supper Lee said to Grace, "Isn't it amazing the difference in the school since Ted came in as headmaster. I mean, Billy Bob and I have been friends for years, but I feel like we have a real leader at St. Bonnie now. Before, I felt Billy Bob was undercutting everything I tried to do. And he never told me I was doing a good job. Ted tells me that almost every day. It's nice."

"I too have noticed the difference," Grace said. She got up and began clearing the dishes from the table. Lee helped her rinse them and put them in the dishwasher.

"The future looks a lot better," Lee said. "For a while there I was thinking about resigning for next year. In fact there were a great many times when I contemplated not even staying till the end of the year."

He came up behind her and put his arms around Grace. "But being with you is the most important thing in my life. Whither thou goest I will go and whither thou lodgeth I will lodge, and thy people shall be my people."

"I think Ruth said that to her mother-in-law, Naomi," Grace laughed. "But I'm glad to hear you are staying."

"I do have another summer project however," Lee said. "I want to do some research and see if I can talk to some of the lawyers in the St. Bonnie family about getting your mother free."

"Oh, Lee," Grace cried out. "I would love nothing better than to have my mother out of that horrible place, but if you talk about it around here, it will get out. No one around here but you and Billy Bob know that my mother is in prison. I want to keep it that way. Promise me you'll keep that quiet."

"Whatever makes you happy," Lee answered, but he was not giving up the idea.

CHAPTER ELEVEN

The trip to State University proved to be a second honeymoon for Lee and Grace, or maybe it was a first. They attended their seminars during the day, then met and had wonderful evenings. One night they even went to a baseball game the university was playing.

"I'd almost be willing to stay here forever," Lee said. "Too bad we didn't know how good we had it when we were in school."

"My memories aren't exactly happy," Grace offered. "Remember I was living with my grandmother. We, that is she, didn't have much money so I had a job in the office of one of the professors. I had to type his letters and record his grades. Sometimes he even let me grade the papers. This was before computers, of course."

"What did he teach?" Lee asked.

"Fortunately, English literature," Grace said. "At least that was a subject which I could understand and make some headway in grading the tests. He always checked after I had graded them, at least he said he did."

"We have to develop a game plan for the coming school year," Lee said. "We or at least, I don't want another one like the one just past. Ted seems to be a reasonable man and from all appearances, he'll be a good headmaster. Are you satisfied with the way he's overseeing your work?"

"I have no complaints so far. But come fall we have the Southern Association's first inspection toward our accreditation. They'll make two or three more trips before its final, but I'd like that first visit to be a positive experience and have them impressed with what we're doing at St. Bonnie's."

"What can I do to help?" Lee asked.

"Work hard on the publicity you're getting out. We are coming along with your three goals, the coed high school, and the fact that we now go pre-kindergarten through the twelfth grade. And, I don't see how anyone can think of us as 'the little school in the church basement' any longer."

"Yes, I bring one or the other of those points, all three if possible, into all the press releases I send out to the newspaper and to the television stations."

"I think we should always put academics ahead of athletics, and I hate to say this, but the wins we have so far on the playing fields have helped establish some of those goals—especially the coed high school."

"What about the girls' teams? Are you planning to do anything about Sweet Ole Brownie's rules for discriminating against females?" Lee looked at Grace.

"I guess I should have told you sooner, but I've already sent a letter to HEW filing a protest against those rules."

"Oh boy," Lee whistled. "That ought to stir up a real hornet's nest. Will that affect Southern's report on us?"

"Who's going to tell them?" Grace said.

"Well, if it's favorable, I'll spin it up and send the news to the whole state. If it isn't, that is if you lose your case, I'll never tell."

"I know you won't. But the whole principle is so wrong. I hope my complaint and my filing a claim will make a difference for the girls who want to play sports."

"You'll always make a difference, Grace," Lee gave his wife a hug.

During the summer the new gym was finished in record time and everyone, students, faculty and parents were looking forward to using it. Basketball would be played there after the volley ball season ended and there would be no more physical education classes in the hot sun or sitting in the lunch room when it rained.

The fall opening assembly and the first faculty meeting had barely dismissed when the weather became a large factor in the new school year. It not only looked like rain, but a hurricane formed off the coast of Africa, then moved into the Caribbean and finally into the Gulf of Mexico. The weather reports said the exact direction of Fannie, the name of the storm, was not known. It could come ashore anywhere along the Gulf of Mexico from Brownsville, Texas to Tampa and St. Petersburg, Florida.

Though it was slow moving, when it began a path straight up the middle of the Gulf, Ted Walker called in all the male faculty and maintenance personnel.

"Billy Bob," he said, "I'm putting you in charge of preparations. We need to board up all the windows we can, get all the items off the grounds that might be flying missiles, make a plan for the days we may have to close the school. Decisions must be made as to when we'll dismiss the students."

"Lee," he turned to face him. "Your job will be to notify the parents and the news media with a written statement outlining our plan. Bring it to me and you and Billy Bob and I will go over it before you send it out."

"Time is of the essence. According to reports, this thing is only about two or three days away." Ted continued. "LeRoy, get over to Home Depot and pick up all the plywood you can buy and start your crew boarding up the exposed windows."

The storm did not change its path and the new predictions showed a hurricane warning from Morgan City, Louisiana to Panama City, Florida with St. Bonnie right in the center of the pointing arrow.

Ted called Lee in and asked if he would be willing to stay overnight in the main school building the night the storm was predicted to hit.

"I'll have to have Grace with me," Lee said at once. "I wouldn't leave her in our apartment alone."

"No, of course not." Ted said. "I'll stay here, too, and maybe we'll get other faculty members who can come to join us."

Fannie seemed determined to pay a visit to the community and area of St. Bonnie. Students were dismissed and told not to return until further notice the day before the hurricane was expected to hit. It appeared Fannie would come ashore during the darkness of night.

Lee went to the grocery store and stood in line with hundreds of people buying flash lights, batteries, bottled water, peanut butter, jelly, cans of Spam and tuna fish, Cokes, and bread. The store shelves were bare of some items, but most customers were in a jovial mood. Some even announced they were preparing for hurricane parties.

At St. Bonaventure those people who would remain overnight came with sleeping bags and blankets; a change of clothes and boxes of non perishable food and many drinks. .

Lee made sure his battery radio was operating properly and

checked to be sure he had spare batteries. Billy Bob brought a flounder light which ran on canned fuel. LeRoy assembled the tools they anticipated might be needed—saws, hammers, an axe, rakes, even a crow bar.

"We'll have the chain saw till the gasoline runs out," he said.

"Can you think of anything else we will need?" Lee said to Grace as they were leaving their apartment.

"Don't ask me," Grace said. "I've never been in a hurricane. We didn't have hurricanes in Kansas, only tornados."

"I'll choose the hurricanes,' Lee commented. "At least we have warning they are coming."

The group gathered in the central hall of the main building, using adjoining rooms for storing the supplies.

"We'd all better be in the hall for the worst of the blow," Ted recommended.

They sat around talking and watching the weather channel on the television they had brought into the area. All the local radio and television stations were broadcasting nothing but hurricane news now, showing the area weather radar and giving a count-down. They repeated the same things over and over.

About ten o'clock in the evening, the power went off. The television died and all the lights went out all over the world, it seemed to Lee. They couldn't see out of the windows of the adjoining rooms because of the plywood which covered them.

Soon the wind began to howl, louder and louder. The shrieking wind continued for the next six or seven hours. Lee thought it would never stop. He and Grace sat together for awhile, and then lay down on the sleeping bags they had brought. But there was little sleeping with the loud noise outside. They heard crashes as flying objects hit the building. The heavy thumps that occurred from time to time were probably falling trees, they concluded.

Finally just before dawn, when the winds sounded less fierce, everyone got very quiet. Grace drifted off to sleep on Lee's arm and he held her close. His arm was going to sleep, but he didn't want to wake her by moving it so he kept still with his muscles feeling like needles were sticking them.

They had long ago turned off the flash lights and radio to save them for what they did not know—for later anyway.

Finally, Lee became aware that light was creeping into the hallway. With all the boarding up, it was not a bright light, but he knew it must be another day. What would it hold for them and for St. Bonnie?

Lee was the first to stir. He walked down the hall way rubbing his aching arm. When he got to the front door of the building, he saw only green--green pine needles. A large pine tree had blown across the door way. Ted and Billy Bob came up behind him, followed by LeRoy.

"Get the tools, LeRoy," Ted said. "I don't think we are going to be able to get out the front door without sawing our way through this."

Ted was right. They sawed and pulled and tugged and finally cleared enough room to step on to the entrance way. The front yard looked like a war zone. Trees were down everywhere. Pieces of roofing were scattered about, some stray lumber, and a swing from some porch somewhere. The old oak tree, Old Annie had succumbed to the heavy wind and lay split in two pieces, one half of which had fallen across the drive which led up to the front door.

Then, as if Mother Nature wanted to add insult to injury, the sun broke out and sent a splash of light and rays across the destruction.

Grace came up behind the men. "Oh, my God," she gasped. "Did an atomic bomb hit?"

"The force of Fannie came close to a bomb," Billy Bob said. "Where do we start to clean this up?"

Ted sprang into action. "Lee," he said, "Get the radio going and see what the area has suffered and what plans are in place."

"LeRoy, get outside and see if you can assess the damage and determine how many men and how long it will take to clean it up."

"Lee, do you have your camera?"

"Yes, I brought it and six rolls of film," Lee said, "its back with my stuff. I'll get it."

"Good," Ted said. "Go out and take pictures of everything now. Once we start to clean up the debris, we will need some proof for the insurance claims of how bad things were when we started. I'd give a pretty penny for a cup of coffee right now."

"Boss," said LeRoy. "I brought us my Coleman stove and a coffee pot. There's some coffee in the teachers' lounge. If you want, I'll brew us up a pot before I go out to begin looking at the damage."

"Great idea, LeRoy, that's my man to think of that." Ted said. "I think we all need a hot cup of coffee to get this day started. Grace, can you check the bathrooms and the lunch room and see if we have running water please? Let's all get some energy first and then we can begin to assess. I don't think this stuff is going to go away."

Lee thought he had never had a cup of coffee which tasted so good. They found some sugar and some dry creamer, and even a pack of cinnamon rolls, a little stale, but everyone ate them with relish.

Finally Lee was ready to go take the pictures. He squeezed out the hole in the pine branches that LeRoy had cut, went into the campus area and began shooting pictures. He took several shots of Old Annie, and then went around the corner of the main building.

The sight ahead of him turned his insides to knots. The beautiful new gym which was going to mean so much to St. Bonnie was a crumpled mass of steel girders, a blown off aluminum roof, and insulation shredded and hanging loose. The rain from the storm the night before made puddles on the new gym floor and in spots around the remains of the building. With a heavy heart, Lee began to take photographs from several angles.

He felt overwhelmed with sadness. They had never even played a game in the new gym. Now it was gone—totally destroyed.

Lee felt heartsick as he wandered about the campus taking photo after photo of the destruction. Trees were down, windows were shattered, and limbs hung in dangerous positions. There was debris everywhere, and Lee dutifully recorded it. He wandered back to the little prayer garden which had been used by the brothers when they owned the building.

After St. Bonnie had taken over the property from the brothers, the students parked their bicycles on racks in an area by a statue of the Virgin Mary which stood at one end of the garden. The statue became known as "Our Lady of the Bicycles." Lee looked at Mary and gave a heavy sigh. A limb of a cedar tree had fallen across the marble figure and from the way it landed it, appeared to be held up by Mary's arms. Lee snapped a photo of it, and then felt compelled to move the branch. "There, Lady of the Bicycles," he said, "That may be a Cedar of Lebanon, but you don't have to hold it."

Lee spent a lot of time photographing the now destroyed gym. The students were going to be so disappointed. Everyone had looked forward to having so many events in the new structure. Lee didn't see anything that he thought could be salvaged. He went to his building that housed his office. Part of the roof was blown off, but he saw that his office, because it was covered by the old stands, seemed to be in pretty good shape. He opened the door and found that some rain had fallen into it. There was water on the floor and his desk had insulation scattered on the surface. Lee was very glad he had taken the laptop computer with him when they were preparing for the hurricane.

Lee took all six of the rolls of film he had brought, and Ted Walker was very pleased. As predicted, the photographs were very helpful several months later when the insurance claims were filed and reimbursement made to St. Bonnie's for the storm damages.

The cleanup took weeks. In fact, it was three weeks before the students were allowed to return to classes. The electric power was off for sixteen days, and it was not possible to have classes with no power. When it finally came back on, it would go off and on during the school day. There was damage on every street in town and to nearly every house in the city. It took hours of labor as tons of debris was hauled away.

Lee and Grace returned to their apartment which was not structurally damaged, but things were a mess. The refrigerator had to be cleaned out and everything in it thrown away. Lee finally got a Coleman stove like the one LeRoy had brought to school the night the storm hit. He and Grace cooked all their meals on the porch of the apartment and went every day to the ice give away to get a bag of ice for the things in the picnic cooler they used.

It was very hot and sticky and Southerners used to air conditioning were hot and sweaty all day and sleeping at night was not comfortable. The houses in the South were no longer built to capture the breezes blowing through, so everyone had to endure the heat and more than that, the humidity.

Lee and Grace were both glad there were no classes being

held. Lee went up to St. Bonnie's every day to help with the clean up. Grace worked at home as best she could, but with no power and no computers, things went slowly.

Ted Walker notified the Southern Association of Colleges and Schools that they needed a delay in the visitation committee. SACS was gracious in granting an extension which allowed Grace more time to complete some necessary and required reports.

Ted Walker broke the bad news to Lee three or four days before the students returned to classes. "Lee, the inspectors say your building has to come down. It is not structurally safe in its present condition and it would cost more to repair than it would to build a new one. We will, in fact, incorporate your office into the new gym. Meantime, I guess you'll have to operate out of the card board box, as some of the teachers have had to do in the past."

Lee had grown attached to his little cubby hole under the stands and rather hated to give it up. The idea of a new office in the new gym had been attractive; now that was months if not years away. He would no doubt be gone before he got a real office. He guessed he would have to bide his time and wait. One of the good things about the New Year was that Lee did not have to coach football. He was still assigned the cross country team, and his public relations and director of development duties kept him quite busy. Everyone felt they were way behind with the school year with the three weeks interruption from the hurricane.

The financial state of St. Bonnie was working against Lee in his quest to get more donations. The entire city had suffered damage from the storm, and business was slow to pick up again. St. Bonnie wasn't losing money like some companies because the tuitions were collected in advance, but there were many new expenses not budgeted and Ted called Lee in and told him to make fund raising his number onc project.

Lee decided he must develop a game plan. The Southern inspection called for one so maybe he could kill two birds with one stone and have a plan for Ted and one for the report to Southern.

He wondered what school policy was considered a "must" take place and what fell under the "shall" take place. Determining that would give Lee more clout in demanding the steps he followed. But he certainly couldn't demand that money be donated. He would have to come up with a plan that would show how donations would add to the better and greater education of the students. He wanted to be sure he was taking care of any current benefits. Some parents had pledged in the past to make monthly donations in addition to the tuition they paid for their children to attend St. Bonnie.

It was a big job but he would focus on the positive. This could be his big chance to get out and do something better. He could expand his network, and update present finances, line up some references and begin to make some calls.

Lee was not at all happy when Ted Walker selected Grace to go on a conference with him and Billy Bob. Lee thought he should have been included, and he didn't like the idea of his wife going out of town to a meeting with two other men. Then at the last minute, Billy Bob couldn't go. Lee never found out why Billy Bob wasn't going. He naturally expected he would take Billy Bob's place, but that didn't happen.

And so now his wife and the headmaster were traveling out of town to be gone for three days. Lee fretted the whole time they were gone. It wasn't that he didn't trust Grace for he did trust her completely. Maybe it was Ted he didn't trust. Lee thought it just didn't look good especially in light of the lectures Billy Bob had given the year before about how all faculty members should be completely above the board in their behavior.

Lee got almost paranoid when he entered the faculty lounge and suddenly everyone stopped talking. He thought they must have been saying poor Lee, there he is and his wife has run off with the headmaster.

They finally returned from the conference and Lee questioned Grace cautiously. He didn't want to sound accusing, and surely, there was nothing for him to worry about.

"Tell me about the conference," Lee said the first night there were back eating dinner in the apartment again.

"Same old seven and six," Grace said.

"Did you learn anything new?" Lee wanted to know.

"Yes, I think it is possible to learn something new every time you go to such an event. At least, if you don't learn anything, it's a waste of time and money."

"Did Ted seem to enjoy the meeting?"

"I guess so. I didn't see much of him. I did wish you were there. First of all, I missed you, and second, they had a good session on fund raising. One of my old friends was there and she told me it was one of the best meetings of that sort that she had ever attended."

"I wish I could have been there, too, for the same reasons." Lee said.

"I was able to get you some hand outs they gave away." Grace offered. "I'll get them out of the things I brought back and give them to you. You will have to wait till Monday, however, as that box is at school."

"Thanks for thinking of me and bringing the hand outs. I'm glad you are home though." Lee felt happy and relieved.

And so the school year finally got going although the effects of the hurricane were evident for many months. Thanksgiving seemed to come quickly and then it was time for Christmas vacation again.

Lee found it hard to realize he and Grace would have their first anniversary during the holidays. He asked her if she wanted to go to Chattanooga again.

When she didn't answer immediately, he added that they could go see her mother in Kansas. He hadn't told Grace but he was still doing research on how to have her case re-opened and perhaps get her mother freed from the prison term.

A couple of days before the holidays began, Grace said something about repeating the same trip again this year. We'll celebrate our anniversary in the mountains around Chattanooga, and then it will be nice if you are willing to go see my mother again.

The drive to Tennessee was pleasant as the bad weather hadn't yet set in. While they were at Lee's parents having the usual holiday dinners and parties, the telephone rang one night.

Lee's father came into the living room and announced that the call was for Grace.

"Who would be calling me here?" she asked as she left the room.

Shortly thereafter, Grace came back to the door way and motioned Lee to come to her side. "Let's go out on the porch and talk," Grace said.

Lee followed her and she shut the door behind her.

"Lee, that was Mother calling. It seems someone got her case re-opened. She has received a pardon from the governor of Kansas. They are going to let her out. She chose two days after

Christmas. She wants me—us–to come get her, and let her come home and live with us until she decides what to do. Oh, Lee, I don't think that will work at all. Do you know anything about this?"

Lee didn't answer and waited to let Grace's words sink in. He hadn't done any real work toward any release of Grace's mother though he had wanted to and done some research into it.

He said that to Grace.

"What are we going to do?" Grace sounded panic stricken. "How can I have my mother come live with us straight out of jail? It will blow St. Bonnie sky high. I will be asked to resign for sure."

"It can't be that bad. We don't have to tell anyone where she's been." Lee tried to sound reassuring.

"I doubt it with the gossip line that circles St. Bonnie. She's liable to tell where she's been herself. Being in that prison all these years will surely make a difference in her personality, her emotions, and her psyche. After all this time of separation, I don't even know her."

"We can't let them turn her out on the street. Where's your sister? Could she go get her?"

"Not likely." Grace frowned. "She's never been willing to help Mother or even go see her. Remember last Christmas?"

"It'll be all right," Lee put his arm around Grace. "We'll see that she is well taken care of."

But now that Grace's mother was going to be released, Lee found he wasn't so pleased after all. Not only would a mother-in-law be in their house, but one who had spent the past many years in jail.

He didn't say so, but he agreed with Grace that it wasn't a very good idea.

CHAPTER TWELVE

Lee and Grace decided the only thing to do was drive to Kansas and pick up Grace's mother. The cost of flying was prohibitive for three plus they didn't want to come back to Chattanooga and have the adjustment and the explaining of Grace's mother to Lee's family.

They set out from Chattanooga early in the morning and drove straight through so they could spend the night in Kansas and be there early the next day when Grace's mother was released.

It was a trying situation for Lee and for Grace, too, he felt sure. They got to the drab gray prison about eight o'clock and were led into a waiting room. Presently Grace's mother was led in with a paper bag containing a few items. Lee wondered if they had given her any money. He also wondered what she had to bring out since she had been in the place so long.

Grace embraced her mother and the warden told them they were free to leave. They walked out into an overcast day with a chill wind blowing out of the north.

"We'd better get on the road soon," Lee said. "I heard that snow was predicted by late afternoon."

They put Grace's mother in the back seat of the car and Lee began to drive. They cleared the city limits before anyone said anything.

"Thanks for coming to get me," Grace's mother said.

"You're welcome," Lee answered. "By the way, what do you want us to call you, or rather what do you want me to call you? Mrs. Garland sounds so very formal."

"I would like for you to call me Elizabeth, for that's my name. Or, better still call me Beth. That's what my mother used to call me."

"Beth it is then," Lee said. He tried to sound cheerful though he didn't really feel much joy at the moment.

They rode on in silence as the miles rolled by.

"Are you good to my Grace?" Beth asked breaking the silence.

"Yes, ma'am," Lee answered. "I love Grace very much, and

I will always do everything in my power to make her happy."

"Sometimes love isn't enough," Beth said and looked out the window.

Even with Grace taking over some of the driving, she and Lee were nearly exhausted and they decided the safest and most sensible thing to do was stop over night in Memphis.

They checked into the Holiday Inn on the edge of town, one that had two king-size beds. Grace and Lee took one of them and gave Beth the other. Lee tried not to feel embarrassed, but he had never been in such a situation before and he didn't know just what to do. Finally he lay down in his T-shirt and pants on the far side of the bed he and Grace had selected and pulled the cover over his head. Grace was soon beside him and the two fell into a deep sleep.

Lee was awakened by Grace shaking him fiercely. "Lee, wake up, Mother's gone."

Lee leaped up and looked around the room. Elizabeth was indeed nowhere to be seen. "Did you look in the bathroom?" Lee asked.

"Yes, the door is unlocked so she must have gone out while we were still asleep."

"Stay calm," Lee instructed. "We'll find her. She can't have gone far."

They hastily threw on enough clothes to go outside their room. No one was in sight. There were a few cars parked in front of some of the units, but no one walking about.

"Let's check the office," Grace suggested, and they hurried down the walk to that building.

"Oh, Lee, where can she be? I knew this was not going to work out, but I frankly didn't expect it to turn sour so quickly." There was panic in Grace's voice.

They entered the lobby of the office area. No one was behind the manager's counter. The clock that hung on the wall read 6:30 a.m.

They looked around frantically. Both stopped abruptly. There sitting on a plastic-covered sofa sat Elizabeth drinking coffee from a paper cup and reading a newspaper.

"Mother," Grace cried and ran to her. "You scared us half to death. Why didn't you tell us you were coming up here?"

"You were asleep. Besides, I'm a free woman now. The

warden told me so. I can come and go as I please. I don't have to tell anybody." Elizabeth spoke with determination.

"Of course you are, Beth," Lee answered quickly as he saw the anger darting from Grace's eyes. "But we're in a strange town and in the future, we would appreciate it if you would tell us before going off. You are free to go out, of course, just let us know where you are going and when you will be back. Grace and I do that for each other so we don't worry."

Elizabeth stared at both of them. "The coffee is good, and it is free. Why don't you have a cup?"

Grace and Lee did have coffee and a doughnut from the tray. Elizabeth took a banana as they were leaving. They were soon in the car again riding down the Interstate.

"I didn't mean to worry you," Beth said after awhile. "You just can't know how good it made me feel to be able to open the door and walk out without finding it locked or some guard watching over me. It was like a whole new world for me."

"We're glad," Lee said. Grace did not say anything.

They got home about dark and fortunately had several more days before school started again. Lee moved his and Grace's desk into the kitchen and made a place in the spare room for the fold out bed he had brought from his old apartment.

"We'll fix this up better for you," Lee explained. "For right now, we will just get you comfortable and we'll all get adjusted." Grace followed Lee around and he wondered why until they had gone into their bedroom, closed the door, and got in bed. Then she whispered, "This isn't going to work, Lee. We aren't going to have a minute to ourselves. We need some time alone. This apartment isn't big enough for the three of us."

"We can't do anything else right now. Surely you can get your sister to help out by keeping Elizabeth some of the time?"

"I'll have to go somewhere else to use the phone. I don't want Mother to hear the conversation. I can't let her think we don't want her—not after all she's gone through."

When Lee got up first the next morning, he peeped into the spare room. Beth's bed was carefully made up. There was no sign of Beth. Lee quickly looked in the kitchen and living room. He even looked on the porch. Elizabeth was nowhere to be found.

Lee let out a breath. This really was going to be a problem.

He and Grace had enough to handle without playing hide and seek with Beth every morning. He went out on the porch and looked down the sidewalk.

There he saw Beth walking along slowly. She pulled a green leaf from a shrub by the side of the walk and turned it over in her fingers. She paused to look at a budding camellia on a bush in a yard nearby.

I guess we can't understand how she feels, Lee thought. She's been behind bars for nearly twenty years. That has to do something to your thinking. And now she can come and go. No wonder it is so attractive to her.

He threw on some clothes and went out the apartment down the walk. He soon caught up with Beth.

"I see you're having a morning walk," Lee said. "Mind if I join you? It is a beautiful day for a stroll."

The two of them walked about a mile further down the street and then turned and came back. Neither said much.

When they got back to the apartment, Grace was fuming. "Now both of you are taking off without telling me where you are going," she said. "We must have better communication if we are going to live together."

"You sound like your father used to sound," Beth said crossly.

Grace drew back and folded her arms across her chest. "Don't ever say that to me again."

"Well, it's true. He used to criticize everything I did, you know."

"No, Mother, I don't know. I can only remember your screaming at each other. I am very sorry for the past few years of your life. That wasn't my fault. Now Lee and I have gone to Kansas to get you; and we will try to help you establish a new life, but you can't keep upsetting us and making make problems."

"Lee was with me," Beth said. "And maybe nothing was your fault in our family disaster years ago, but let me remind you that if I hadn't done what I did to protect you, you might not be alive today, or certainly not the dean of academic affairs at this prestigious school. You owe me something."

"I don't owe you a thing," Grace shouted. "Because of you I had to spend my childhood with my grandmother. I had no normal childhood. Now when I'm trying to help, you are determined, it seems to see that I don't have a happy marriage. I'm going to call my sister and see if you can stay with her awhile."

"I should have known you would try and get rid of me as soon as possible. Why did you come get me if you were only going to throw me out in the street?"

Lee jumped into the argument. "Let's all be calm now," he said. "Surely we can work something out here. We can be glad to have you, Beth, and you can be glad to be here. I know it's crowded for three people in this small place, but we have to work on a solution, not quarrel about things."

"So what do you suggest, Lee?" Grace turned to him.

"Let's fix some breakfast and give ourselves time to think." Lee went into the kitchen and put the coffee on. Grace followed soon after and got out some eggs and bacon which she began to cook. Beth disappeared into the spare bedroom and didn't come out until they called her to come eat breakfast.

They sat at the table eating silently. Lee said, "I've thought of something. My old apartment is vacant because my lease still hasn't run out. I'm paying the rent on it anyway. Grace and I stored some things there until the lease expires. Beth, you can live there, and we'll all have room to move about more and get our lives back to normal. What do you all think of that?"

The two women looked at each other and then at Lee.

"That might work," Grace said. "How would you like that, Mother?"

"A place of my own? A real apartment? Could I come and go without phoning you every time I go to the grocery store or the drug store?"

"Certainly. You'd be welcome to visit us here, to come for visits and meals, but that way we would all be able to move more freely." Lee smiled for it seemed to him that he had solved the problem.

"Yes," Grace nodded her head affirming the idea. "If you are willing to do that, Mother, we'll help you get the necessary things to set up housekeeping in Lee's old apartment."

"I'd like that," Beth said quietly.

It didn't take as long as they thought or as much buying as they anticipated. Lee had left all his cooking utensils, enough sheets and towels, some furniture and a dresser and chest of drawers. They needn't have worried about that space as Beth had no clothes to put in anything anyway.

Grace took her mother shopping for some new outfits, they visited several charity shops and Beth's new living quarters began to take shape. Lee moved the bed from the spare room back to his old apartment for Beth and his computer and desk back to the spare room office.

As the New Year rang in, it seemed that things would be happy after all.

CHAPTER THIRTEEN

The school term began to unfold into the new year. Things were going smoothly with Grace's mother living in Lee's old apartment. She checked in with them frequently, at least daily, and came over to have a meal with them several times a week. Lee and Grace had no idea what she did during the day. They had provided her with a small television set and they supposed she watched the soap operas, CNN, or The Weather Channel.

Since she had no car or drivers license, there was no danger of her driving away to unknown parts. Paying for setting her up for living in Lee's old apartment pushed Lee and Grace's budget. Elizabeth had no job skills to put on a resume. Lee wondered what would happen if she made any application, and was asked for any crime or prison record. Not many businesses were willing to hire a convicted felon. That would wipe out Beth's chance for any employment and any supplement income.

But, as long as no one was rocking the boat, they let things ride. There had been no occasion to announce that Grace's mother was now living in town. Lots of people had mothers who lived in town. Lee decided to adopt the theory that if it ain't broke, don't fix it. He would rather give up some things than have Beth back in their house, and he was very glad she was out of prison–that was for sure.

One Monday morning Ted Walker called Lee and Grace, along with two other faculty members, to his office.

"We have a problem," he said to them. "Some parents are threatening to sue the school for discrimination against their child. That's all I know. I have no idea what kind of discrimination it is, but when they come in for a conference with me, I want you people present as witnesses. We will call the group the School Support Committee and you are each a member. I'll let you know when the meeting is set up."

"Will the parents be willing to have us sit in on their complaint?" Grace asked.

"They will have no choice." Ted replied. "I will tell them such matters are heard by our School Support Committee."

Lee didn't think about the meeting again because he had a lot of duties as athletic director being sure all the birth certificates for St. Bonnie's student athletes were on file with the High School State Athletic Association. He knew Sweet Ole Brownie had not forgotten Grace's challenge to him. He let it be known he was not pleased she was still at St. Bonnie's. Lee knew he was out looking for any thing he could find to disqualify St. Bonnie's from athletic competition. He had to be sure all contracts were signed for various athletic contests and that everything was in perfect order.

Ted met him coming in one morning and said, "The Student Support Committee will meet at ten o'clock this morning. Those parents I told you about are coming in. I've already told Grace and the others. Be in my office just before ten and we will have the meeting with the parents, Mr. and Mrs. Horace Mathews. The child's name is Annie and they also have a boy in the school whose name is Mark.

Ted Walker opened the adjoining door from his office to the conference room and the committee members all sat around one side of the circular table. They left three vacant chairs on the other side for the Mathews family who entered quietly.

"We are here to discuss your claim—I mean your problem for the time being." Ted began when all were seated. "We have here the School Support Committee who will study the situation and make recommendations. We would like for you to begin by describing your complaint of discrimination."

Mr. Mathews spoke first. "Our daughter, Annie, has been treated very badly by members of her eighth grade class. We feel what has happened to her is the worst form of discrimination. We would like for you to hear her story in her own words."

Annie was a plain looking girl about fourteen years old. Her expression was that of a deer caught in the headlights of an automobile. Her blond hair was pulled back in a pony tail and her pale blue eyes had a frightened look. "Can't you tell them?" she pleaded, looking toward her father.

"Now Annie, we have discussed this before. It will be much more effective if you will tell Headmaster Walker and the committee what happened to you. Please go ahead."

Annie cleared her throat and began. "It started before Christmas when the girls that I thought were my friends said I couldn't sit at the table with them in the lunch room any more. My feelings were really hurt because Betty, who has been my friend since we were in the fifth grade, seemed to be the one who had turned against me the most. Then they all stopped talking to me and ignored me if I tried to talk to them. They said I didn't belong in their group anymore because my parents weren't rich. Betty and her parents aren't rich either, but that didn't seem to make any difference to them."

Annie sniffed and looked at her hands.

"Go on," her father urged. Annie's mother looked as stricken as Annie did.

"Then they began to tell lies about me," Annie sniffed. "They said I shoplifted in the mall stores, and that I cheated on tests, and that I told lies about them. Mr. Walker, That's not true! I never did any of those things, Girl Scout honor. The more I denied what they were saying, the more lies they made up. I was so miserable. When I sat in my classes, I couldn't concentrate because they were laughing and sneering in the back of the room. My grades began to slide, and I couldn't think of anything but how to make them stop teasing and tormenting me."

"Did you tell your Mother and Father what was happening?" Grace asked.

"No ma'am, not at first," Annie murmured.

Mrs. Mathews spoke up. "I knew something was wrong because Annie was not being herself at all. It took me a long time to get her to admit what these girls were doing."

"If they found out I'd told my mother, they would make it even worse," Annie said.

"What happened next?" Ted Walker asked.

"All of a sudden they got real nice and talked to me and asked me to sit with them and I thought everything was going to be all right." Annie got out a tissue and wiped her nose.

"I guess it wasn't or we wouldn't be here," Lee spoke up this time.

"It seemed to be back to where it was," Annie said. "They invited me to a Christmas party at the home of one of the girls. They said everybody was coming, that it would be a really nice party, and I should get a new dress for it."

Mrs. Mathews interrupted. "Although we couldn't afford a fancy party dress, Annie seemed so happy to be included again that we went shopping and bought her a dress that cost far more than we could afford. I was pleased to see Annie her old self again so I thought it was well worth the cost."

"The day of the party I took Annie to the beauty salon to get her hair fixed. She put on the new dress and she looked so pretty and she seemed so happy. We decided that I should take her to the party and come and pick her up later when the party was over. It's about a forty-five minute drive from where we live to the house where the party was to be held. I got her there and let her out of the car. All the children were milling about in the front yard and they greeted Annie as she walked up. I pulled off in a happy frame of mind thinking my child was now accepted and would have a good time at the party. You tell them the rest, Annie."

"They gathered around me and waited until Mama got out of sight," Annie said. "Then they began to laugh and laugh. The boys slapped each other on the back and they roared with laughter. 'You stupid hick, they said, 'Did you really think we would invite you to one of our parties?' That was what they said, and worse, and the girls joined in, and they laughed some more. Then they all together said, 'There's no party, dummy, we really fooled you didn't we?'"

And they got in some cars and drove away and left me standing there in the front yard of the house.

"I didn't know what to do. Mother had not had time to get home. I finally knocked on the door of the house and a nice lady came and let me in. By then I was crying so hard, I could hardly tell her what was the matter. I finally told her there had been a mistake, and I had come to the wrong house for a party and could I please call my mother."

Mrs. Mathews spoke. "I walked into my house to hear the telephone ringing." Annie was in tears and begging me to come get her at once. So I got right back in the car and drove the forty-five minutes to the house once again."

"Annie rushed out to the car as soon as I pulled into the drive way, sobbing as if she would cry every tear in the world. I got out to thank the kind woman who had let her wait in her house and use her telephone. She did not have any idea what was going on. Annie cried all the way home and cried herself to sleep."

Mr. Mathews spoke next. "Since that night, Annie has refused to come to school. I think that a school which operates under the auspices of St. Bonaventure Church should be teaching a few Christian principles. It's been a financial struggle for us to keep Annie and her brother in St. Bonaventure, but we felt they were getting a good education. Now we don't like what they are learning in the least."

The School Support Committee looked around at each other.

Headmaster Walker spoke. "What do you want us, that is the school, to do about this situation?"

Annie blurted out, "I will never go another day to this horrid place."

"Shhhh," her father said. "We are going to withdraw both Annie and Mark from St. Bonaventure. We expect a full tuition refund for both of them, and a satisfactory recommendation on each of their transcripts. We want St. Bonaventure to call the guilty students together and make them apologize to Annie—in front of the whole student body."

Ted Walker leaned back in his swivel chair. "We will discuss your request and get back to you."

"We'll give you forty-eight hours," Mr. Mathews said, "Or else."

"Or else what?" Headmaster Walker looked straight at him.

Mr. Mathews stood up and locked eyes with Ted Walker. "Or else we will bring suit against St. Bonaventure for discrimination, child abuse, and cruel treatment of our daughter by other students. I personally will call the local newspaper and tell them exactly what happened. The recent parent newsletter says St. Bonaventure has applied to be accredited by the Southern Association of Colleges and Schools. I will write a letter to Southern Association as well and tell them exactly what happened. That ought to serve to call their attention to how this school is run."

He turned to his wife and Annie. "Let's go," he said. "We've told what happened. What happens next is up to you and this committee. We'll see what you do in the next two days and then take whatever action we need to."

The Mathews left the room.

The committee members looked at each other and then to Headmaster Walker.

One of the committee members said, "What do we do now,

Coach, punt?"

"This is ridiculous," Walker said. "That was just a childish prank. Teens do things like that all the time. It's part of growing up."

"I can't agree with that," Grace said. "It was indeed a cruel act, deliberate, mean-spirited, and hateful. Something like that can affect a child for life as it well may have done."

"We can't ask the students involved to apologize," Walker insisted, ignoring what Grace had just said. "I don't know just who these students are, but some of them are bound to be children of some of our most influential parents. It will ruin St. Bonnie if I ask those people to do such a thing as apologize before the whole student body."

"We need to do the right thing, Ted," Lee insisted, "Regardless of the social status of the guilty students."

"Great," Ted Walker said. "You're public relations director. You handle it then, but no calling the students for apology. Let me know how you solve it."

"All right," Lee said and got up and left the room.

CHAPTER FOURTEEN

I have what is known as disaster control," Lee said to Grace as they came into their apartment after the school day had ended.

"I think it is Ted's place to handle this," Lee went on. "He's the headmaster."

"That's why you are public relations director," Grace said. "You are the fall guy. Either you fix all the disasters, as you call them, or it is your entire fault, not theirs. Speaking of which, do you have any idea what you'll do?"

"I got the distinct feeling there is no way Ted is going to call the guilty students for an apology. We don't know who the guilty students are and there's no possible way to identify them. I'm sure they aren't going to volunteer to come forward. I can understand Ted not wanting to take the flack from the most influential parents in St. Bonnie when we're just stabbing in the dark. The girls set it up, but I'm sure those boys present were in on the hoax as well."

"I have an idea," Grace said. "Why don't I call Annie Mathews into my office that is if she'll come, and talk to me? Maybe if she feels better about the whole thing, her father won't be so adamant about bringing suit or calling up apologies to further embarrass the victim and the perpetrators."

"It's worth a try," Lee said. "Because right now I have no idea what to do. They use the Tylenol poisonings as an example of good disaster control, but that won't fit into my situation here."

"It's just a different kind of poison," Grace added.

The next day Grace called Annie Mathews, who had not been back to St. Bonnie to class. "Annie," Grace began, "This is Grace Garland, dean of academic affairs at St. Bonnie. Would you be willing to talk to me alone about the party which never happened?"

"Yes, ma'am," Annie said. "I know who you are. I've seen you lots of times at St. Bonnie. I will talk to you, but we will have to do it somewhere besides at school. I meant it when I said I would never set foot at St. Bonnie's again and my parents are backing me on that."

"I could come to your house," Grace offered, "But I'd like to talk to you by yourself and if we are at your house, your parents will probably want to enter the conversation so it won't be just you and me. What if you met me at the Frosty Ice Cream Shop this afternoon about four o'clock? I'd like to buy you a sundae and just have a woman to woman talk."

"That will be fine. I'll meet you there." Annie agreed.

The two females got to the ice cream shop on time and took a booth near the back of the room. Grace had the feeling Annie didn't want to be seen talking to her, but that was all right with Grace.

They both ordered hot fudge sundaes and began to eat them.

Grace began. "Annie, I am so very sorry about what happened to you. It was a cruel and thoughtless thing for those boys and girls to do, and I don't blame you for not wanting to be with those people at St. Bonnie's anymore. When they asked you to the party, you had no idea that they were going to pull a joke on you, did you?"

"Now that I think more about it," Annie said, "Some of them were laughing when they asked me, but I was so excited to be included and to be asked, I didn't think anything about it. Then every day they'd ask me if I was really coming. They asked if I had got a new dress, because, they said, it was a real dressy party. I guess I should have known something was phony then, but I didn't. I was too happy to be accepted again. "

"Do you want to tell me who the ring leaders were? Who kept asking you these questions?"

"Oh, all of them," Annie said. "You know who they are. The social snobs of St. Bonnie. They think they're better than anybody else. They judge people by the clothes they wear away from school because we have uniforms here. They decide if your house isn't in the Country Club neighborhood, you are a nobody. They think the rich people are the only ones who matter. But my daddy pays the same tuition at St. Bonnie as their parents do."

"Life is certainly not fair," Grace said, "And I know it doesn't do any good for me to say that even if it's true. But there's another saying, 'What goes around comes around.' One day you will see that you are a bigger person than those who would mock you and do terrible things like the party that never was."

"It might have been something I did before they started asking me to the party," Annie said.

Grace raised her eye brows. "Really, what was that?"

"My brother Mark was going to St. Bonnie, too, you know. He is one grade ahead of me, but he's not started growing as much as I have and I'm bigger than he is right now. Well, one day after school when everybody was waiting for their rides, some of the boys started picking on Mark. One of them, Boris Meany was really nasty and got up in Mark's face and called him bad names and kind of pushed him. So I grabbed Boris and punched him in the jaw and knocked him down. About that time one of the teacher monitors came walking towards us and the boys all ran away. But I think maybe Boris might have put the girls up to the party idea to get even with me."

"Did you tell your parents about this?" Grace asked.

"No, Mark said to keep quiet. He said they had been picking on him all year, and now that his sister had knocked one of them down with a fist to the jaw, they would make his life even more miserable. Should I tell them now and get Mark mad at me? He won't be going back to St.Bonnie either, so I don't think it will make that much difference and my daddy is mad enough as it is."

"Is it important to you to have those guilty apologize in front of the student body assembly?" Grace studied Annie to get her body reaction as well as her verbal one.

"Daddy is pretty insistent that they do that, but I don't care one way or the other. What difference will it make? They surely won't ever accept me whether that does or doesn't happen. It would only make things worse for me and for Mark. I just don't want to go back to St. Bonnie again ever."

"What do you want to do when you grow up, Annie?" Grace asked.

"Well, I had thought about becoming a veterinarian because I love animals. But I just couldn't put one to sleep even if it would be the kindest thing. So I have decided I want to be a police officer."

"That's an interesting career. What made you decide on police work after you decided against being a vet?" Grace took another bite of her sundae which was beginning to melt.

Annie shrugged her shoulders. "I only decided that recently," she said. "I want to be a police officer and be in the traffic division. I'll drive around in the police car and look for drivers who are speeding or driving recklessly."

"And then what?" Grace wondered if Annie would say what she thought she would.

"One day," Annie said, "When I'm a traffic officer on the police force, I will stop one of those people who were at the party, or one of the girls who asked me and then teased me about a new dress will run through a red light in her big SUV. It was hard for my mother to buy that new dress because it was expensive, and I didn't get a new dress very often. Anyway, one of these days, I'll stop one of them or one of the boys speeding down the street in their BMW convertible. I'll sock them with a traffic violation, and I will charge them with the most and the biggest fine possible. I'll look them in the eye and say, 'You remember me, I'm the one you invited to the party that never was. Now here's a ticket for you to the traffic court and a hefty fine. I hope it makes your car insurance go up even higher. Have fun at court—it's no party." Grace couldn't help but smile. What goes around, comes around, she thought.

"Well, Annie, I appreciate your meeting with me. I certainly sympathize with you, and I don't blame you for feeling as you do. And, I hope you get to be a traffic officer and do have the pleasure of stopping one of those thoughtless people when you have the upper hand. But right now, you are definitely sure you and Mark will not return to St. Bonnie?"

"I'd rather kill myself than go back there," Annie slapped her hand on the table.

"Don't say that, Annie," Grace begged. "We'll be sorry if you don't return. The faculty and lots of students aren't like those others. But if you aren't coming back, why doesn't your father just drop the demand that they apologize?"

"I wish he would, but you don't know my daddy. When his mind is made up, it is made up and there is no changing him." Annie finished her sundae and leaned back in the booth. "I'm enrolled in the public school district where we live and Mark and I will be starting there tomorrow. Thanks for the ice cream and for being nice to me. At least someone at St. Bonnie cared enough to talk to me about this."

"I wish it were otherwise," Grace said as they left the booth and she stopped at the cash register to pay for the sundaes. "Good luck in your new school, and let me know when you get to be a police officer. I know you'll be a good one."

Grace reported the essence of the conversation to Lee that night. "I really feel so badly for Annie," she said. "That was a cruel and indecent thing to do to a thirteen year old girl. This is such a sensitive time of life and other children can be so cruel, especially those who are the "haves" versus the "have-nots." Neither Annie nor Mark is coming back to St. Bonnie. That's for sure. She told me they would attend the public school near where they live. But, she also said her father was not one to change his mind. So if the students involved don't apologize, and we could never be sure we had all of them, Mr. Mathews may bring that suit and notify the newspaper as he threatened."

Lee listened carefully. "So we will lose the battle and the war, too," he said.

"Looks that way. I did what I could." Grace signed.

"I'm glad you talked to Annie. I hope it made her feel better. You have a way of making a person feel better, you know," Lee smiled at Grace and gave her a hug.

The following day Lee reported to Ted Walker. "The two Mathews children have withdrawn and are going to attend public school," he began. "We can't determine exactly which students were involved in the faux party; some of them were probably hangers-on anyway. Nothing will be accomplished by contacting parents when we can't say their children were responsible. They will only say 'My children would never do that.' So I don't see how there can be any apology or what good it would do if it did take place. We might try to get some faculty involved in teaching kindness and consideration along with social studies or something. Maybe we ought to get an eighth grade award for doing nice things. Nothing is going to undo this particular episode."

"We'll just close the book on it then," Ted Walker said and got up from his desk chair indicating to Lee that the conversation had ended.

Monday morning St. Bonnie received notice that the school was being sued for character assignation and discrimination by the Mathews family.

CHAPTER FIFTEEN

Ted Walker stormed through the halls causing several students to jump aside and shake their heads. The headmaster was definitely upset about something, they reasoned.

He roared into Lee's quarters where Lee had been making do while the new gym was being constructed.

Ted threw the door open so hard it bounced into the wall and swung back nearly hitting Ted.

"What kind of public relations person are you?" Ted yelled. He threw the notice of suit on Lee's desk. Lee turned slowly and scanned the document then looked at Ted.

"So they decided to sue anyway," he said.

"You're damn right they are suing. You were supposed to stop that in its tracks. What have you been doing to let this happen? I thought you were taking care of it." Ted got red in the face as he raised his voice.

"Hold on a minute, Ted," Lee said. "I've been doing everything I could to appease the Matthews, but there is a limit to what can be done when a parent thinks his child has been hurt—and Annie was definitely hurt all right. What those kids did to her is inexcusable."

"I don't want to hear about what was done to Annie. Your job was to make things right and you certainly haven't done that. What is your excuse? Not that it will make any difference now that this has happened."

"I offer no excuse," Lee stood up. "This was a ticklish situation from the beginning. The little girl snobs of the eighth grade did a terrible thing to a human being. They had been tormenting her for weeks before that only we didn't know about it. Did you know Annie decked Boris Meany for picking on her brother?"

"What's that got to do with it? They are suing us; can't you get that through your head? This could cost the school a bundle. In public relations it can tear down everything we've done since we got the new building and began our push as a high school. Our military school competition will eat us alive, not that they don't do the same thing there. This could cost me my job. It could cost you your job. What are we going to do?"

"I'd suggest we contact our legal counsel right away," Lee said and he sat back down. "If they have filed suit, we have to deal with that to go forward. It does no good to say 'what if' now."

"You can be sure I'll tell the lawyers that you were directed to stop the threat of a suit and you didn't do it." Ted Walker turned on his heel and stalked out of Lee's office.

Lee waited until he thought Ted was a distance away and he got up and went immediately to Grace's office. She was talking with a student so Lee had to cool his heels and wait in the outer office for them to finish. Finally the girl came out of Grace's office.

"Come in," Grace said, "What's the matter? Has Mother escaped again?"

"No, not that," Lee took a deep breath. "It's really hit the fan. Ted Walker just left my office in a state of a near stroke. It seems the Matthews have brought suit after all. He accused me of being at fault because it happened. What the hell could I do that I didn't do? You talked to Annie. The kids have withdrawn from St. Bonnie. Ted was the one who wouldn't ask the snobs for an apology, although I agree with Annie that calling them out would have been the worst thing we could do. Things would have gone from bad to worse if we'd done that. This is just a teen age prank, terrible though it is, but Ted says he might lose his job over it. Worst than that, he says I may lose mine, too, not that I'd care at this point."

"Sit down and stay calm," Grace said. "Let's think this through. What do our school lawyers say about it?"

"Apparently he came to me first and hasn't even contacted them." Lee sighed.

"Well, the thing to do is ask the legal opinion. Our hands are tied now. There is nothing either you or I can do at this point. Surely Ted is just overwrought. He can't think he'll lose the headmaster job."

"Don't be too sure of that," Lee said. "Don't forget the parents of these children are the ones who raised them. With their attitude of 'My child would never do that', we won't get any support from them."

"I guess there's nothing more to do but wait it out," Grace said. "Have they carried out the rest of the threat about calling the story to the newspaper?"

"Oh my God," Lee moaned. "I haven't even thought of that. My bet is that Matthews will go all the way with his threat. I'll call my buddy Bob Reading at the paper and see if he knows anything about it."

Lee went back to his office and put through the call. Bob was out on a story so Lee left a voice mail to call him back as soon as possible. Lee didn't state the nature of the reason for the call.

The dismissal bell had rung when Bob called back. "Hey man," Bob said. "What the hell are you guys doing out there at St. Bonnie?"

"What do you mean by that?" Lee asked, knowing full well what he meant...

Susie Snoop, you remember her, she does the living section which used to be the Social Page, well she got a hold of a rumor from St. Bonnie about how they mistreated students who weren't in the rich and social crowd. Y'all wouldn't mistreat any student, would you?" Bob laughed.

"She isn't going to run that kind of story, is she?" Lee felt his neck muscles tighten.

"Hard to say," Bob suddenly got serious. "You sound like it might be true. Susie is checking the facts, but I think she may run it if she finds it's true. It is a good story you have to admit; and, best of all, do you know that Susie Snoop's daughter was refused admission to your Kindergarten a few years back? They said the class was full, but Susie never believed that, and she's had a chip on her shoulder for St. Bonnie ever since. Boy, I'd say y'all have got a problem out there."

"You've told me what I want to know. Thanks," Lee said. "I guess there's nothing left to do but hold our breath and read the paper."

Lee told Grace about the conversation at home that night. They agreed there was nothing they could do. They decided to splurge and go out to dinner, and they chose the best restaurant in town and ordered a bottle of wine as well.

"Here's to the future, whatever it may be," Lee said and tapped Grace's wine glass.

Lee got up early and got the newspaper from their front door. He rattled through the front page section, and then turned to the Metro News. There on page three was the whole disturbing story.

He went inside with the paper and sat with Grace drinking their morning coffee. She read over his shoulder.

"Susie Snoop got the story pretty straight, didn't she?" Grace said, "But I can't believe she'd print it, even phrased as it is as just gossip."

"Vengeance of a scorned mother," Lee said. "I wonder what the real reason for not letting her child in Kindergarten was, not that it matters now."

Susie Snoop had not mentioned any names which was a great relief to Lee. And, if she knew about the suit, she didn't say so as it was not mentioned either. But printing the story was sure to hurt St. Bonnie. The school already had the reputation for being a snob school and as Ted Walker had said, the military rival was going to pump this for all it was worth to prove they had the superior school though they were just as snobby if not more so than St. Bonnie. Though the military school was older and had been at it longer, that made no difference in this matter, Lee thought they would only rejoice they hadn't had students act in a similar fashion.

Lee and Grace slipped in the back door of the school that morning not wishing to discuss Susie Snoop's column with any other faculty.

Ted Walker was sitting in Lee's office chair when Lee got in. Lee got angry this time. No job was worth this. He had done his job in acceptable fashion, and there was no cause to blame him for this whole miserable thing.

"Did you think of any other solutions over night?" Ted was sarcastic in his question. "You had all night to think of something."

Lee paused before answering. He hasn't seen the morning paper, Lee thought. But he will see it, and then what?

"What did our lawyers say?" Lee asked.

"Same thing lawyers always say, 'it depends'. They said they'd have to study the facts and investigate the case."

Lee decided doing anything was better than doing nothing and sitting there while Ted blamed him.

"Depending on what the legal experts say of course," Lee began. "My suggestion would be to settle with the Matthews out of court. The last thing we want is to get in court with this thing. Offer to refund the Mathews' tuition in full for the year for both the children. Send a written apology from the school, and see if that will do it. If the thing ends up in court, it will go on and on, and the bad public relations will only get worse. Give them back their money," Lee said. Tell them to go to hell, Lee thought but did not say aloud.

"Maybe that is the best idea," Ted said and left the office which both surprised and relieved Lee.

To say it hit the fan when the faculty and student body read the news article was putting it mildly. The students cut out the article and stuck it on every bulletin board they could find. They inserted vulgar and obscene remarks and pasted those clippings on the lockers of certain students. Of course no one could catch the guilty parties though everyone had a pretty good idea of who was doing most of the postings.

This went on for about a week, then it suddenly died a natural death. Ted Walker met with the legal arm of St. Bonnie and recommended a settlement out of court. The lawyers agreed this was the best way to quiet things down.

Lee never found out the total price paid to the Matthews but he suspected it was more than the tuition amounts alone. But whatever it was, the talk died down and the social snobs tormented the kids from the other side of town again and the worst thing was, they got by with it again. Lee sighed and thought that was something that would always be part of being a teenager. Human nature just couldn't be changed, he thought.

Ted Walker never gave Lee credit for his suggestion that the matter be settled out of court, but he also said nothing about anyone losing his or her job. Lee wondered what that meant, but was grateful and went on with his every day assignments. He worked up a new resume, however, just to be ready in case. Again, he began to wish he was away from St. Bonnie's.

The job loss came from another direction. One night shortly after the suit was settled, they got a call from Grace's sister, Karen. They didn't hear from her often so a call meant something was wrong or she needed money.

"I'm coming to stay with y'all awhile," Karen announced. "Our company got bought up by another corporation and my job got phased out. Freely translated, that means the person doing my job with the other company gets to keep the job and I'm out."

"Don't they have something else you can do in the new set up?" Grace asked. It was she who had answered the phone.

"No, and I'm ready to get out of this town anyway," Karen said. "I'll see you in a day or two."

"Karen, I'm sorry you've lost your job, but your coming here will pose some problems," Grace said.

"We'll work them out when I get there," Karen said and she hung up.

CHAPTER SIXTEEN

The fanfare regarding the suit and the bad publicity in the newspaper eventually died down, but to Lee's way of thinking, things did not get back to normal. Things certainly weren't normal in their home life either.

Grace's sister, Karen, arrived with bag and baggage and moved into the small apartment and took over. She was the messy one while Grace was the neat one, but it didn't take long for the whole house to look like the proverbial hurricane had hit it.

Grace and Karen didn't get along very well either. Grace stayed in a bad mood, and Lee gave up trying to mediate between the two sisters. Then there was Mama who decided to visit much more often since both her daughters were together.

Lee and Grace had little time by themselves and mostly had to conduct their private conversations at school.

"Grace, we have to do something to get Karen out of our house. I can't stand it much longer," Lee announced one morning as they sat in Grace's office.

"You're right. I'm not any happier than you are about the situation," Grace said. "I know it's tough to lose a good job, but Karen whining about it all day doesn't change anything. She needs to get out and get a new job."

"She needs to get out of our house," Lee sighed.

"She's coming to eat lunch with me today. I'm going to suggest she move over to Mother's," Grace said. "They deserve each other."

Lee was working on a news release for the upcoming Parents Day when Ted Walker came into his office. Ted said, "From now on, I want you to bring all your news releases to me before you send them to the paper,"

"Is there a problem? Are you not pleased with them?" Lee asked.

"They seem awfully short and lacking in detail," Walker said.

"Then I'll gladly bring them to you first so you can see how much the paper cuts from what I send them. That's par for the course, you know. They like to say it's because they need the space for something else. Usually the something else is a paid advertisement."

"Just bring them to me." Ted walked out.

Karen began to come to school for lunch every day which further rankled Lee. Was there no getting away from this woman? Karen dressed in the latest fashions and began to make friends among the faculty. One day she was called in to substitute for a sick teacher. The crowning blow for Lee came when Karen came and ate lunch with Ted Walker almost every day. The days they weren't in the lunch room, Lee suspected they were eating in a nearby deli.

"Good news," Grace said to Lee at their apartment one night. "Karen has agreed to move in with Mother."

"What does Mother think about that?" Lee asked.

"It doesn't matter what she thinks, we're paying the rent. I hope Karen will get a job soon, and then she can take over some of the expenses."

"It can't be too soon for me," Lee sighed.

A week or so later, a faculty meeting was held at St. Bonnie's. Ted Walker got up smiling. Lee thought of Billy Bob and his "I guess you wonder why I called you here today" remark. He actually wished for Billy Bob to be in charge again. Lee wondered why Ted had called them as it was not time for the regular monthly faculty meeting. He soon found out.

Ted got up and began to speak. "This won't take long, and you'll be out of here on time. I want to introduce you to our new director of Public Relations, Miss Karen Garland."

A round of clapping followed. Lee sat stunned. Ted had not said one thing to him about a new public relations director. He had come and asked for the press releases before they were delivered to the newspaper, but a new director?

Ted was speaking again. "I hope you'll give Karen your complete cooperation. And be sure to call her every time you have an event that is suitable for the newspaper or the television stations. We hope to get some good publicity from now on." He looked straight at Lee.

Lee was drinking a glass of merlot when Grace got home that evening. She came over and gave him a hug and kiss.

"I've been shot out of the saddle at St. Bonnie's," Lee said. "Ted Walker doesn't ask my opinion on anything anymore. Used to be, when Billy Bob was in charge, I was consulted about matters. Now I'm totally out of the loop. I don't like the feel of this or the implication. Hiring Karen as PR director without even telling me is the height of insult. To let me find this out in a faculty meeting with all the other St. Bonnie personnel was not a nice thing to do. What qualifications does she have to be public relations director anyway?"

"Lee," Grace began. "I know you're upset. I would be, too. Ted didn't tell me about the hiring either, and of course, Karen wouldn't tell me. As for her qualifications, I don't know. She was a district sales manager for her old company which I don't believe has much to do with public relations. But look at it this way, she has moved out of our apartment, she'll have some income so she can take over the rent at Mother's apartment and maybe it will be best all the way around."

"Best except for my future at St. Bonnie's," Lee grumbled. He poured himself another glass of wine. "But then I never had any future there anyway."

Things didn't get any better for Lee at school. He was no longer allowed to work independently. Karen was in his office constantly asking what he was doing. Lee also realized she was using him as a crutch. She didn't know much about public relations, and she asked Lee to write nearly all her releases claiming she was busy with other things and didn't have time. Lee did as she asked but only for Grace's sake and only for a little while longer, he thought.

Karen went around with a camera and took pictures of everything. She would then ask Lee to send them to the newspaper. Lee knew that things like a birthday party in the Kindergarten class were not considered newsworthy by the paper and that they would not be used. She insisted he send them anyway, and when they did not appear in the paper, Karen would question Lee about whether or not he had really sent them. Lee did submit them, but he was more and more embarrassed as he knew his reputation as a good provider of real news was being endangered by sending in 'fluff', as he called Karen's stories and pictures.

When word came that the Southern Association of Colleges and Schools was finally coming to have the first inspection of St. Bonnie's, Karen rushed into Lee's office and told him they needed to get a news packet ready to give the committee members.

She actually confessed to Lee that she had never done a big press release with statistics, photos, mission statement and other vital data.

Lee stopped what he was doing and spent the better part of the day assembling all the details to make up the packages. He had to go out and buy folders because Ted had refused his purchase order previously to print up a supply of such folders with the school photo on the front and pockets inside to hold extra flyers and the like. At the time, Ted had said it was too expensive.

Now Lee had to use plain folders which he thought reflected poorly on the school. He got the twenty-five required packets ready and took them to Karen's office. He cringed every time he had to go to her office as it was one of the nicer corner offices with a view of the front campus.

He left the folders on her desk and went into the hallway just as Ted Walker entered Karen's office. Lee could hear the conversation inside as the door was open.

"I got the news packets ready for you," Karen purred.

Lee felt the blood rise in his throat. Then he heard Ted say, "Great job, Karen, that is just what I wanted. This will help us with the accrediting of St. Bonnie's. I knew I could count on you to do this right. Thanks a million."

That sneaking bitch, Lee thought. I spend all day on those damn things and she takes the full credit and never even mentions my name or the fact that I did all the work.

Lee fumed about it all afternoon, but he decided not to tell Grace what had happened. He was also feeling that Karen was not only putting a wedge between him and Ted Walker, but between him and his wife. Karen was, after all, Grace's sister and though they were very different personalities, thank God, they were still blood relatives. Lee decided to suck it up and keep quiet for awhile anyway.

Was it Lee's imagination or were his co-workers and faculty members tending to avoid him? The usual chatter in the faculty lounge ceased when Lee came in. Other faculty members did not ask his advice on things as they once had. Am I going to be ignored completely from now on? Lee wondered.

Lee decided to confront Ted Walker. It took him two days

to get an appointment to see Ted. When he finally got in and was seated before the headmaster, Lee found he didn't know where to begin.

"What's on your mind, Lee?" Ted asked.

"I don't know what my job description is any more. You have brought Karen in and she is supposed to be doing public relations."

"Supposed to be," Ted interrupted. "Didn't you see the marvelous job she did on the packages for the Southern Committee?"

"I saw them all right," Lee snapped. "I guess she didn't tell you I helped her get that information together."

"Come on, Lee, don't try to take credit for Karen's fine work on that project," Ted said.

Lee swallowed his anger. He felt he was beating against a stone wall. Nothing he said, apparently, was going to change Ted's attitude toward Karen, or toward him as far as that went. "Will she be doing the development and fund raising, too?" Lee finally asked.

"In time, yes, meanwhile, you keep that going and let's see if we can raise some money. Why don't you get another fund raising letter ready? Bring it to me when it's finished and make it by Friday, will you?"

Ted got up and escorted Lee to the door.

Lee, old buddy, he thought to himself, you surely can see the handwriting on the wall here. Ted is pushing you right out the door of St. Bonnie's. You had better polish that resume some more and get it out. Your experience and expertise are no longer wanted or sought here. You're a has-been, old buddy; recognize that and do something about it. Let's get the hell out of Dodge and leave this place.

Lee went home early and collected the mail from their box. He took it inside and was flipping through it when he came to a letter to Grace from the Department of Health and Welfare in Washington, D. C.

Wonder what this is? Lee thought. Maybe an answer to Grace's complaint about the girls' athletic team rules? It had been months since she first filed the complaint. Were they just getting around to it?

Lee was tempted to open the envelope but he couldn't do

that to Grace. It was her letter and her project. He paced about the house wishing she would hurry and get there. Finally he heard the front door open and Grace came in.

"You got a letter from HEW," Lee said. "Maybe they finally read your protest and are answering."

Grace tore open the letter and read for a few minutes while Lee stood by, anxious to know what the letter contained.

"Well," Grace said, "They are investigating my protest. They have a list of things I'm to send them. They want the State High School Athletic Association handbook which contains the rules with the discrimination against the girls high- lighted. They want me to write what amounts to a brief on what happened at the state indoor track meet. They want a list of the sports teams we offer for the female students and the number of girls who participate in each sport. It will take me awhile to assemble all this. Can you help me do it, Lee?"

"Of course, I'll do anything you want and need," Lee smiled at Grace. And, he thought, maybe for once my work and experience will be appreciated.

It took longer than anyone thought it would to assemble all the data that the department of HEW requested from Grace Garland. Lee helped as best he could and even went to the local newspaper for some research. As he filtered through the many old news and feature stories in the library at the Local Gazette, he dreamed of a day when all the material could be assembled on a computer and accessed with the flip of a key on a keyboard.

He went to the newspaper so many days that he began to have coffee with the city editor, Robert Reading, better known as Bob. When Lee explained to Bob what he was researching and why, Bob became very interested.

"We'll want to run a big feature on that when it fully develops," Bob said. "It was one thing to pass Title IX of the Civil Rights Act in 1973, but putting it into practice here in the South; especially in the heart of football country full of good ole boys is quite another thing. I have a three year old daughter, and I certainly want her to have equal opportunity in athletics if she wants to participate. You have a tough job going against Sweet Ole Brownie, but I guess you know that."

The letters and phone calls went back and forth between

Grace Garland and Washington, D. C. She communicated with an especially helpful black female lawyer. The lawyer and Grace seemed to be in a similar wave length and the lawyer was helpful in suggesting certain tactics Grace should incorporate into her arguments to get the rules on a level playing field. They were on a shared mission with great respect for each other.

Ted Walker called Lee in for a progress report one day. "Lee, you usually do a fairly good job, but today I'm going to have to give you a negative feedback. You just aren't getting the donations into our fund raising project. Can't you get out another letter encouraging more giving?"

Lee wondered why this performance review was necessary at this time of the year. Usually such matters were discussed in the spring when the next year's contracts were being signed.

"Sure. We can get out another letter," Lee said. "But don't you think that would be over doing it? Our tuition was raised for this school year and people can take just so much."

"Just get another letter out without complaining so much," Ted said. "At the rate you are not performing, I will have to assign your fund raising duties to Karen Garland along with her public relations position."

"Coaching takes up a lot of my time, so if you want to do that, it is fine with me," Lee could not keep the disgust from his voice.

"Don't push me, Lee," Ted said. "Anyone can be replaced. And by the way, what is this rumor I hear about your spending so much time at the local newspaper?"

"It's not a rumor. It is a fact. Grace and I, Grace especially, are trying to get the state high school athletic association to change the rules for girls sports so that they are more equal, so that the girls have a more level playing field. I've been doing some research on previous news stories to make our case with HEW."

"You weren't hired to do research on girls sports, Lee," Ted fiddled with some papers on his desk. "Just do the job you are supposed to be doing and let those things solve themselves. And let me have a copy of your new fund raising letter by the end of this day."

Lee left the office of the headmaster both angry and discouraged. He no longer knew what was expected of him—as always. What he was hired to do at St. Bonnie was so far from what he was being directed to do now that there was no comparison. He totally disagreed with nearly everything Ted Walker was proposing these days. Lee considered going to Billy Bob to get his opinion and reaction, but he seldom saw his old college friend. He also had a sad feeling Billy Bob would side with Ted.

Lee wondered what his workplace rights were. He even wondered if he would or could collect unemployment if he were dismissed. No, he didn't think that would happen. What he really thought lately was that Ted Walker would keep up the Chinese drip torture until Lee resigned. Then no unemployment claim was possible.

Regardless, Lee went to the newspaper library one more time. He had been hot on the trail of a Texas case which he hoped to wrap up. Then, since Ted insisted, Lee would stop his research at the newspaper.

He gathered all his research and gave it to Grace to send to Washington. "We've done all we can," Grace said as she wrapped the package and taped it securely. "Now the ball is in the HEW court."

"Do you wonder if Sweet Ole Brownie has gotten word of what you are doing?" Lee handed Grace some packing tape.

"If he had, he'd be calling Ted Walker to fire me for being a trouble maker," Grace laughed. "But I don't care. I'm doing this for the girls, the present teams and the girls to come."

"Ted gave me a poor performance report today," Lee said. "He seems to have it in for me. He scrutinizes every move I make. He even told me not to go to the newspaper library any more. Guess it's a good thing we finished our research there before he issued that edict."

"You're doing a good job," Grace said. "There's no reason for him to give you negative reports. Hasn't it helped to have Karen take over the nitty-gritty parts of public relations?"

"Yes, I am glad I don't have to go to the lower school and take pictures of the kids painting pumpkins and then try to get the newspaper to use such a story," Lee said. "But I'm getting tired of Ted being on my back every time I turn around. I'm leaving St. Bonnie's at the end of this year—that is if I get that chance. The way things are going right now, Ted Walker may push me too far before school's out. He couldn't think I'm threatening to him. I certainly don't want his job. If you will remember, I never wanted to be a school teacher in the first place. I don't even have a teaching certificate. I don't think Ted knows that right now, but if he finds out, I'm sure to be toast."

As Lee and Grace were preparing to go to bed, the telephone rang. "What now?" Lee said, and picked up the instrument.

"Hello, Karen," he said so Grace would know who was calling. "Why are you calling this late?" He almost asked if there was some breaking news that needed public relations attention. He still felt he did most of her job, but for the sake of peace in his own household with Grace, he tried to keep his thoughts on that to himself.

"She what?" Lee said. He covered the mouth piece with his hand and turned to Grace. "Your mother isn't at home. Karen doesn't know where she might be."

Grace grabbed the telephone. "Why didn't you call us sooner?" she asked. Grace talked a few more minutes, and then hung up.

She turned to Lee. "Karen went to dinner with Ted Walker. When she got home, Mother wasn't there. She has no idea where she might be or even where to look. What shall we do?"

"I guess we'd better start looking or calling around, if we can decide where to call," Lee said.

"We'd better call the police," Grace said.

"Too soon," Lee said. "They won't do anything about a missing person report until the person has been missing at least forty eight hours. Do you have any idea where your mother shops? Is there some place she might go? Has she gotten in any bridge groups or canasta clubs?"

"You know as much about that as I do," Grace said. "As far as I know, she does nothing but sit around the apartment all day long watching soap operas. Karen isn't there much so I'm sure Mother gets lonely. Where could she be, Lee, it's after eleven o'clock. Something bad could have happened to her, something terrible. What can we do?"

"Do you know of anything that might have upset her?" Lee was concerned, too, and he didn't want to deal with this problem, not after the day he'd had at school and the talk with Ted Walker.

"She's been upset ever since we brought her from Kansas," Grace mused. "I can't blame her. I'm sure staying behind bars as long as she did does something to your morale and your personality."

"You stay here in case someone telephones," Lee said. He put his clothes on. "I'm going to walk the distance between here and my old apartment where your mother and Karen live. Your mother may have decided to walk over here. She does that often, you know. Maybe she has stopped somewhere en route. I'll call you when I get to the apartment and let you know what I've found." Or not found, he thought, but he didn't want to upset Grace further.

Lee went out of the house and started down the sidewalk. Nothing moved in his vision except a stray cat that jumped up on a fence and stared at Lee.

"Hey, cat," he said. "Seen any stray mother-in-laws around here?"

The cat hissed and jumped behind the fence and scurried off. In a few blocks, Lee came to the Irish tavern on the corner, Paddy's Irish Pub. Lee thought of going in and getting a drink. He felt he needed and deserved one.

On impulse, he decided to go in and ask Paddy if he'd seen Beth.

The lights were low and the bar was about half full. An Irish ditty was playing on the stereo, and there was a murmur of conversation. Blue smoke from cigarettes floated over the booths with an occasional laugh. Lee adjusted his eyes to the dim light and looked toward the bar and Paddy. As he did, he caught a glimpse in one of the booths.

There sat Elizabeth Garland, swirling a drink and deep in conversation with a man sitting across from her. Lee rushed over to the booth.

"Beth," he cried, "We've been looking all over for you. We were worried. Why didn't you let us know where you were?"

"Lee, hello," Beth said. "Sit down". She slid over in the booth. "I want you to meet someone. This is my friend, Sean O'Toole. Sean, this is my son in law Lee Castleberry."

"Pleased to meet you," Lee mumbled. He turned to Beth. "Do you know what time it is? Nearly midnight. Grace and Karen both are worried sick about you."

"I'm so sorry," Beth said. "I didn't realize how late it was. Sean and I get to talking and the time flies. Why don't you join us in a drink?"

"Let me call Grace first and tell her where you are," Lee said. He got up and went to the pay phone on the far wall.

Grace answered on the first ring. "Have you found her?"

"Yep," Lee answered, "I found her all right. She was down at Paddy's Irish Tavern drinking Tullamore Dew with a new boyfriend."

"I don't know whether to be furious or relieved," Grace said. "At least she's all right. I'll call Karen and tell her."

"I'll offer to walk Beth home," Lee said, "But I have the feeling the new boy friend, his name is Sean O'Toole, will want to do those honors. Go on to bed, Grace, I'll see to this and be home shortly."

Lee replaced the phone on its hook and went back to the booth. He sat down by Beth and said, "Now I think I will have that drink. After all that's happened to me today, I need and deserve a drink."

He ordered Tullamore Dew on the rocks.

CHAPTER SEVENTEEN

Grace and Lee and Karen, this time in a different mood, met over supper the next night to discuss the new boy friend of Elizabeth Garland.

"I think it's wonderful," Lee said, "It will give her some social outlet and take her mind off all those unpleasant memories."

"I just wonder if he's taking advantage of her. Does he think she has money?" Karen asked.

"He can ask all he wants, but that won't create any fortune for Mother." Grace said. "I agree with Lee that having a boy friend will do her good. After all, she is still a good looking woman, and she can be charming company if she puts her mind to it."

"I guess we can stop asking where she is going and when she'll be home," Karen added. "The parent child role reversal is no more. She is a woman of her own mind, and since she is over twenty-one, she can damn well do as she pleases. We will just have to wait and see what develops from this."

Lee got a phone call from Robert Reading the next day inviting Lee to join him at the monthly meeting of the Public Relations Council of Alabama. Lee jumped at the chance to do some networking and maybe put an ear to the ground for a position since his number one priority now was to get out of at St. Bonnie's.

Lee had been a member of this club in past years and remembered it as one of the most productive memberships he had ever had. He learned more at the meetings at that time and felt that the contacts he made were the most beneficial of any group in which he had ever participated. He had thought of reinstating his membership when Billy Bob first appointed him to director of public relations at St. Bonnie, but then all the other jobs came up and before he could concentrate on being public relations director, Karen had the title, so he hadn't pursued it.

Now he had a chance to see what had transpired during his time away from the group. About fifty persons were gathered in the dining room of the Seaside Trade Club and Lee saw a number of people he had known previously. He greeted them and told him his present position. He carefully worded things so he could say he had gone to St. Bonnie's as public relations director. He neglected to mention he had been relived of that job, time enough for that when he heard of a particular opening and could apply for it.

"Are you out at the little school in the church basement?" one of his old comrades remarked as he joined the group.

"Yep, I am at St. Bonnie's," Lee said and he thought he hadn't done such a good job after all with his goal to set a new image of the school.

"I wouldn't think St. Bonnie was big enough to need a public relations director," the friend said..

"Well, you know in this business, we always think everything we do creates an image in the community." Lee said.

"Well, you sure shut the door on the bad publicity that was resulting from the family suing for discrimination," Bob Reading commented.

"Teen age actions," Lee hastily added. "You can't stop the cruelty of that age group, but we tried to silence it." He was glad when the buffet food line opened and the members began to fill their plates.

Lee and Bob took their food to a round table and sat with several other PRCA members. The conversation drifted off to non-profit public relations. Lee realized a much larger number of non-profit organizations were represented in the club now than there had been when he attended previously. He wondered why, but then thought to himself that, after all, St. Bonnie might be considered non-profit. He had certainly emphasized the fact that contributions to the school were tax deductible for those who chose to itemize their tax returns every April.

Lee and Bob had ridden together to the luncheon and as they drove back to the newspaper office where Lee had left his car, Lee told Bob he was thinking of leaving the school and going back to commercial work, maybe public relations or maybe he would even consider newspaper work.

"I thought you liked school teaching," Robert remarked.

"I never ever wanted to be a school teacher," Lee said. "If I didn't have the public relations and coaching, I would have been out of there long ago. You know my wife is dean of academic affairs and now my sister in law has come to work. Getting to be too much nepotism. Besides, I get tired of things like the teenage problem we have. Today's kids are different and the parents get involved. They expect teachers to take over part of their parenting duties so they can go to the country club and play tennis or golf. I'm getting burned out, so I thought I'd look around the real world and get out of the ivory tower if I can."

"I'll keep an ear to the ground for you," Bob said. "If you'll send me some hot news tips—not that stuff you've been turning in."

"I know, I know," Lee said. "I didn't want to send it, but the boss man doesn't know the real meaning of public relations. He thinks it's getting column inches in the paper no matter how dull and boring the story might be."

Lee was getting out of Bob's car and about to go to his own when he stopped and turned to his friend.

"It's a little early, but I might have a good lead for you soon," he said.

"Not another picture of the landing of the Pilgrims," Bob laughed.

"No, something really big. My wife Grace, you know the one who is dean of academic affairs, well, she was coaching girls' indoor track last season, and there was a conflict with Sonny Brown, executive director of the state high school athletic association. He pushed Grace's button the wrong way about the different rules for boys and girls track and she filed a grievance with HEW. They have recognized her complaint and asked for a bunch of data which we just sent to them this past week. If HEW comes through and tells Sweet Ole Brownie he has to change the rules or lose any federal funds that might make a big splash for you."

"It ain't going to happen, old buddy," Bob said. "You don't mess with Sonny Brown. You weren't in the school business a while back when a group of tennis parents challenged Sonny. He had a rule that the high school tennis players couldn't play for their schools and play any other tournaments during the high school season. That went over like a lead balloon. You see, the players get their rankings from the Southern Tennis Association tournaments, and some of them are very serious about those rankings. If they didn't play in the Southern tournaments in the spring, then their rankings suffered in the summer circuit play. So the players had to choose between playing for their schools or playing the Southern tournaments. You know what the players chose and the high school teams suffered because the good players weren't participating. The parents wanted both so they complained to Sonny. He let them know real quick that he was the boss and what he said was the law. That rule didn't change."

"Well maybe the Federal Government intervening would make a difference," Lee said. "After all when federal funds are involved, people sit up and take notice."

"You got a good point there," Bob said, "And if HEW does answer your wife's complaint with any edicts, it would be a big story. Keep me posted, you hear?"

"I'll do that," Lee promised. "Thanks for the lunch, and let me know if you hear of any job openings."

When Lee got back to St. Bonnie's, he was confronted by Ted Walker.

"Where in the world have you been?" Walker asked. "I've been looking for you all day."

Lee wondered if Ted had nothing better to do than look for him all day.

"I left word with the receptionist that I was going to the Public Relations Council of Alabama luncheon," Lee said. "What do you need me for?"

"Why are you going to the public relations lunch?" Walker asked. "Karen should be taking care of that. You know it's her job now."

"So you told me," Lee said sarcastically. "My buddy from the newspaper asked me to join him there for lunch. I didn't see any harm in keeping up good relations with the news media."

"Next time you want to leave the campus for lunch, ask me first," Ted Walker said. He turned and walked away, and Lee wondered again if he had wasted his time looking for Lee all day. What was his gripe? Lee was back in plenty of time to teach his journalism class, the last period of the day. Lee decided the frequent run-ins with Ted Walker were not a good sign. He determined to increase his search for a new job.

Friday night Lee and Grace invited Karen and Beth and her new friend Sean O'Toole to come to dinner at their house. Karen declined saying she had other commitments. Lee suspected she was going out with Ted Walker but didn't mention that to Grace. The way Ted had been treating him lately, all he needed was to get between Ted and Karen, his sister-in-law. That could only make things worse.

Beth was happier than Lee had seen her since they went for her in Kansas on her release from the prison. He had tried to imagine what it must be like to be behind bars for days on end, years on end, and he was happy that was now behind her.

Lee and Grace both were very pleased at Beth's new attitude on life. And it was doubtless because of Sean O'Toole. Lee splurged and bought a bottle of Tullamore Dew and they all sat around the living room with their drinks as dinner was cooking.

Sean was funny and Lee liked him immediately. He had been a semi-professional baseball player when he was younger and filled the conversation with stories from his playing days. Beth hung on his every word and smiled. Lee hadn't seen her smile for weeks so that, too, was a good sign.

Grace had cooked corned beef and cabbage in honor of the Irish. Sean had an Irish name and Irish ancestors, but he had been born in Brooklyn and never even been to Ireland.

"One day, though," Sean said, "Me and my Beth are going to make that trip."

My Beth thought Lee and looked at Grace who was apparently thinking the same thing.

Beth and Sean left soon after dinner was over.

"Do you suppose he's going to spend the night?" Lee said to Grace as the older couple walked down the sidewalk.

"If Karen is there, I would think not," Grace said. "But then I wonder if Karen will be there? She's getting mighty thick with Ted Walker, or have you noticed?"

"I've noticed all right. Things are getting worse between me and Ted, Grace. I don't think he'll be offering me a new contract, so I've put out some feelers for another job."

"What's he done now?" Grace asked.

Lee told her about the conversation they had had when Lee returned from the lunch. "He's going to have to define my job description better if I do stay," Lee said. "I don't know where I stand; I don't know what I'm supposed to be doing. Every day it changes and nothing I do pleased Ted. It's a lose-lose situation."

"Surely you are imagining some of this," Grace said. "Don't get paranoid on me. I think Ted's been a good headmaster since he came to St. Bonnie's. He sure knows what to do to get us ready for the Southern inspection."

"I guess that's why he was hired," Lee said. "After all, that Southern accrediting is the most important thing St. Bonnie can have right now. It will make a lot of difference when our high school graduates apply for college. And, it won't hurt to be one of the few independent schools in the state with Southern accreditation."

"But you may be right about the nepotism," Grace said. "Three from one family may be too much for Ted and for St. Bonnie's as well."

CHAPTER EIGHTEEN

The exchange of letters and phone calls between Grace and HEW in Washington grew faster and more furious.

"I can't decide if they intend to do something about this or if they are just stalling and going around in circles," Grace said to Lee. "I've sent them everything they have asked for, some of it more than once."

"Think of what you are doing for the girl athletes of St. Bonnie and the state and America as well," Lee said.

Then one day an envelope arrived. It contained a brief letter to Grace thanking her for bringing to their attention the injustice done to the girls who played sports in the state of Alabama and stating that they were enclosing a letter to the state superintendent of education with a copy to Sonny Brown.

Grace had to sit down to read the epistle to Sonny Brown as it was seven pages of single spaced type. She called Lee to come hear her read the results.

In a nutshell the letter to the superintendent stated that the state and the executive director of high school athletics were to change the rules for participation in sports for boys and girls to read the same. One paragraph told Sonny Brown that if a young lady wanted to pole vault, he was to bring her a pole. The rules in track were to read exactly the same for girls and boys. The same applied to basketball. In the case of tennis and golf, if there was no team for the girls, then girls were to be allowed to play on the boys' teams.

Over the seven pages, single spaced, the letter was very specific about these rulings. "You are ordered…" the edict read over and over. The orders were to be put into effect immediately. Should the superintendent and the executive director of the high school athletics association defy these federal edits, then federal funds would be withheld from the entire state until compliance was made with these directives.

"Wow," Lee said when Grace had finished reading the letter. "There is no doubt about their meaning. What do you think will happen now?"

"Oh, I think the state will comply. They wouldn't dare risk the loss of federal money," Grace said and she re-read parts of the letter. "They have done everything I asked them to do. I suppose Sweet Ole Brownie will call Ted Walker again and ask that I be fired for being a troublemaker."

"You're beyond his control," Lee said, "Be thankful you're in an independent school system that puts you out of his clutches."

"He could make things hard for us with Southern accrediting though," Grace said. "I think I have to watch my back at all times."

"I promised Bob Reading at the newspaper that I'd let him know any developments in this case. Is it all right with you if I call him?"

"Let me talk to Ted first," Grace said. "Then you can let him know."

Ted Walker was not as enthusiast about the news from HEW as Grace would have hoped. "This is going to get us some more adverse publicity," Ted whined. "I wish you'd asked me before you took these steps."

"Making life better and fairer for girls and women is going to get us adverse publicity?" Grace was shocked at his attitude. "This ought to boost us in the eyes of our students, their parents, and the whole community."

"You don't know the old boy network," Ted said. "There are a lot of men throughout the country, especially here in the South, who don't like intelligent, uppity women. They want to keep women in the kitchen barefoot and pregnant."

"Well, I've got news for them," Grace stood up to leave. "Us intelligent uppity women are not going to sit still for that any more. You'll see."

Lee called Bob and met with him to give him a copy of the seven pages, single spaced letter from HEW.

"Wow," Bob said, "This is hot news. I'm going to give it high headlines on the front page, not just put it in the sports section."

And he kept his promise. The newspaper hit the streets in the morning, and the telephones at St. Bonnie began to ring. For the next three days, the story made headlines. By the fourth day, the board of trustees at St. Bonnie called an emergency meeting. Grace was to attend the meeting and explain how the matter had developed. Lee was not among those asked to attend, but Karen was. This only made Lee more determined to get out of St. Bonnie for good. He sent out six more resumes that day.

Grace reported the agenda of the meeting and the reactions from board members. "Some of them were very receptive," Grace said, "Especially those who have daughters in the school. Others obviously were not especially pleased with the HEW report but reluctantly agreed it was probably a good thing."

"What surprised me though," Grace continued, "Was the reception to the Southern Association progress. It seems pretty positive that St. Bonnie will be accepted for admission and accrediting in that organization. This will, as you well know, boost St. Bonnie's reputation by leaps and bounds and should attract a lot more new students."

"Another thing that surprised me," Grace said, "Was how Ted Walker was not very supportive of anything I had done. He wasn't exactly hostile, but he certainly didn't pass any laurels my way. If it hadn't been for Karen being there, I would have felt I was on my own against the whole board. Then things began to swing. The board voted unanimously to commend me for my work toward the Southern accrediting and to issue a special thanks for getting the athletic rules put on a level field for the girls who participate."

"Ted had a negative comment to both motions, but then Charles Cook, chairman of the board, and the one who has a daughter in our school, told Ted that he needed to watch out for micro-managing and that shut Ted up pretty quick."

"What do you think will happen now?" Lee asked.

"First things first," Grace said. "Southern will be here next week so we need to be sure that comes off as it should. After that I'll see that everyone involved knows the new rules for girls playing by the same rule book as the boys. I wonder how long it will take Sweet Old Brownie to get out a revised rule book."

The committee for the Southern Association arrived and for two days they moved about St. Bonnie's, poking their heads into classrooms, talking to faculty, and talking to students. They were in Grace's office half a day checking all the academic offerings and test results from SATs, ACTs, and other national tests. Grace told Lee later that she thought they had come out very well on the academics. "They will make some recommendations, but overall, I think we passed with flying colors." she said.

Lee wrote the news release when the announcement came several days later that St. Bonnie had indeed been received and accredited by Southern Association. Karen took the credit, of course, as she did for the press packets Lee again assembled for distribution. Lee tried not to complain to Grace about Karen's actions. He hoped to be gone soon and there was no reason to bring a rift between himself and his wife.

The newspaper sent a photographer and a reporter got statements from a number of people. Ted Walker was quoted as saying, "I have put a lot of energy into making this school the best in the state. My hard work, and that of others here, has paid off for us. We are happy to be accredited by Southern Association as it will benefit our school and our students as well."

"Nice of him to give you credit," Lee said to Grace before dinner that night. They were getting ready to go to Beth's for the meal. Both of them had been pleased over the great positive change Sean O'Toole had brought to Beth. She was cooking again, getting out more and a pleasure to be around.

Beth had prepared a traditional Southern dinner for them. She had fried chicken, mashed potatoes, English peas, and a tossed salad. She had even made sweet tea and a banana pudding. The four of them enjoyed the meal. As usual, Karen was out with Ted Walker.

"They're getting mighty thick, aren't they?" Beth asked Grace.

"They have a lot of things pertaining to school that they need to discuss and there isn't time during the day to do that," Grace said to her Mother. "I think it's good that she has someone to go out with, don't you?"

Lee remained silent but he was thinking that the headmaster was slowly pushing him, Grace's husband, out of the loop. That didn't matter to him now since he had received several encouraging offers for interviews.

"We're saving to go to Ireland," Sean announced. "We're going to do that for our honeymoon."

Lee and Grace looked up in surprise. "You're what??" they asked in unison. "When?"

"Oh, not for awhile," Sean replied, "But Beth is the girl of my dreams, and we plan to spend the rest of our lives together as soon as we can afford it."

Lee's thoughts went to the apartment where they sat at this very minute. Lee was still paying the bulk of the rent though Karen contributed some now that she was working. I'd welcome you spending the rest of your life with Beth if you will take the financial responsibility for her, Lee thought.

As they were walking home after the meal, Lee said to Grace. "No more idle talk," he said. "It's time for me to get out of St. Bonnie. I'm getting some interest in my resume now, and I expect some interviews soon."

Grace walked on without comment. Finally she said, "I can see how you feel about the way you are being treated at St. Bonnie. It isn't right for Ted Walker to cut you out of everything. You have done so much for the school and you deserve recognition. But we can't control how Ted acts so I can't do anything but tell you to pursue those other positions. I'll miss having you at St. Bonnie; but we have to think about what is best for you, and for us, I will support you in whatever you decide to do."

"I know I can count on you," Lee took Grace's hand and they walked on. "You know that from the start I haven't wanted to be a school teacher. It was a pay check in the beginning; but when you came into my life, it was worth it. Then when I began to be somewhat happy with the job, circumstances began to change. Now I feel like everything I try to do is met with opposition from Ted Walker. I would be glad to go back to the days when Billy Bob was headmaster, but that isn't going to happen."

"You never know," Grace said, "I was surprised at the board of trustees meeting when some of the members locked horns with Ted over some issues. He may not have the support of the board he thinks he has."

"Was there any indication he might be replaced?" Lee asked. "That would certainly make a tempest in the teapot at the place."

"I think Ted misunderstands the power of the board," Grace said. "He's very egotistical about his influence. He practically came out and said the Southern positive visit with us was the result of his efforts when every member of the faculty and staff had more to do with that success."

"You're being modest, dear wife," Lee said. "Without your input we would never have passed the inspection from Southern."

"I don't know if the board knows that," Grace said, "But maybe getting the rules changed for the girls sports has got their attention as to what I, the intelligent, uppity woman, can do."

Lee thought a long time afterward about the events of the ending of the school year; he was amazed at the way things meshed together. At the time, everything seemed crazy and it appeared that nothing would ever be sane again, but it was strange and much like *Tale of Two Cities*, it was the best of times and it was the worst of times.

In thinking about it, Lee decided it began with the rumors. In spite of Billy Bob's repeated instructions and requests about squishing gossip, there was never a time when rumors weren't flying in the teachers' lounge. There were always clusters of people in one corner or the other talking in whispers. When teachers came over from the lower school or the middle school divisions, they got in the corners and the buzz continued. Lee didn't ever trust the rumor mill, but he decided that where there was smoke, there must be a fire somewhere.

What Lee heard was that Ted Walker was leaving at the end of the year. There was a lot of speculation as to who would take his place. Would it be Billy Bob again? The only sure thing Lee knew was that it sure wouldn't be him as he didn't intend to be there for the next term. Maybe Grace was in the running. She had some strong support from several of the board members because of her shaking up Sonny Brown and the rules for the girls' sports. A lot more girls had come out for softball and the track team was very large. St. Bonnie also had a quality tennis team of both boys and girls and two good golf teams made up of both sexes.

Then, too, it had been Grace who led the team which resulted in the Southern accreditation. Yes, Grace might have a chance if she weren't an intelligent uppity woman, Lee thought. But he was very proud of his wife and in his heart he was pulling for her. But he kept quiet. He had no other option.

About that time Lee got a call from Bob Reading saying there was an opening at the paper for a feature editor.

"Are you interested in that?" Bob asked.

"You bet I am," Lee answered.

An interview was set up and Lee thought the talk with the senior editor went well. Lee told him the first job he had ever held, when he was in high school, was at the local newspaper in the town where he grew up. He had a college degree major in Journalism with a minor in English which was the usual requirement for a position such as the one being offered. And, he had plenty of varied experience.

The senior editor talked about thirty minutes, then asked Lee to bring in some of his work, including the several articles Lee had had published in some national magazines in the past. Lee left thinking it was a "don't call us, we will call you" situation, but overall he felt pretty good about the interview.

He told Grace about it that night. As always, she was encouraging.

"What rumors are you hearing in the faculty lounge?" Grace asked. "When I walk in there, the place clams up like teenage girls at a slumber party when one of the mothers appears at the door of the bedroom."

"About the same thing happens to me," Lee confessed. "Although I have heard your name mentioned as the next headmaster, or rather headmistress."

"That will never happen," Grace said. "Besides, I'm not sure I want it to happen. I could get trapped in the Peter Principle, you know."

"Something is definitely going on with Ted Walker," Lee said. "He has ruffled the feathers of some board members and some of the influential parents as well."

At semester's end, Lee was assigned to proctor a final exam. Everyone had to do a shift of it and it was another one of the things Lee hated about teaching. Most exams were held in larger rooms or the auditorium. It was Lee's luck to draw one of the smaller math classes held in a regular classroom.

He passed out the exam papers and then stood in the front of the room. He would walk around, as per instructions, to the back of the room and up and down the aisles. Lee was so bored he almost didn't see one of the girls pull a slip of paper out of her sock. Lee paused a minute to see what she did with it. The girl slipped the paper under her exam and looked out the window as if nothing had happened. Lee was alert now and he zeroed in on her every action. When he saw her copy something from the slip to her exam, he went to her seat and picked up both the exam paper and the slip that had come from her sock.

"As soon as your teacher comes in to answer any questions from you, we are going to the office of the headmaster," Lee said. The girl turned crimson red and started to protest. "Shhhh," Lee demanded. "This is an exam period."

Presently the regular teacher came in and Lee pulled her aside and told her what had happened. He showed the teacher the exam and the cheat sheet and said the student had pulled it from her sock and used it on the test.

"I'll take her and the papers to the headmaster," the regular teacher said. "You keep on proctoring. I'm really not surprised. I've suspected she cheated on some of the tests during the semester. She can never work a problem at the black board, she doesn't get her homework right, but then she scores high on tests. We'll see what Mr. Walker thinks of this action."

She motioned for the girl, who was now in tears, to follow and the two left the room. The rest of the long hour and a half, the other students glared at Lee and stuck out their bottom lips.

When the bell rang to end the exam period, Lee was met outside by the regular teacher who collected the exam papers Lee had taken up. "Mr. Walker wants to see you in his office," she said.

What a surprise, Lee thought and went on upstairs to the headmaster's office. He expected to see the guilty student there but only Ted was in the room sitting behind his big walnut desk as usual.

Ted Walker greeted Lee with an unhappy face. "Here you go again, Lee," he said. "Why must you always be the knot in the rope? Why do I always have to go behind you and clean up the messes you make?"

"I don't know what you mean? I caught the girl cheating," Lee said angrily. "She deserves a zero on the exam, which will probably make her flunk the course for the semester."

"It wasn't that big a deal," Ted said. "Lots of students cheat these days and we never catch them. I read just last week about how many college students are cheating these days. Seems to be the latest trend. Here at St. Bonnie's we don't want to make an example of a high school student like this girl. Her folks will be down on me like a duck on a June bug if we pursue this thing. Let's just drop the whole matter."

"What about the character and integrity in St. Bonaventure's mission statement?" Lee asked. "Cheating is an absolute violation of everything we are trying to teach in this school. We can't just ignore cheating."

"We're going to ignore it," Walker said. "I have instructed the regular teacher to give Shirley whatever grade she earned. There will be no zeros given."

"What she earned?" Lee was shouting now. "I won't allow you to do this. I'll report this to the board."

"Do that, Lee," Walker sneered, "And you and your wife both will be out of a job. I am the headmaster at St. Bonnie's. I make the policy, and I say this girl will not be given a zero. She says she wrote the paper after the exam started. She says she never pulled anything out of her sock."

"Anyone who will cheat like that will also lie," Lee said. "Leave Grace out of this. As for me, I'll gladly get out of your hair. I no longer want to be associated with the hypocrisy that is coming out of this office. You are brown-nosing the rich and famous and letting them get by with anything and ignoring the problems like the one with the Mathews children. The other students know what happened. You are worried about the reputation of the school. Wait till this gets out."

"Karen will take care of that," Ted stated. "Thank heaven I put her in charge of public relations. That will be all, Lee. I have made my decision."

Lee went to his office and began to collect his possessions. With tender care, he took the laptop he had been given by Ben Baker's parents and put it in carrying case.

He collected other items and loaded them into his brief case. He would not be around to get the beautiful functional office in the new gym which was nearing completing. I could care less, Lee thought. I've had enough of this place.

He was so angry and frustrated at Ted Walker he didn't remember he and Grace were to eat supper that night with Beth and Sean at the Irish Tavern. This was one of the nights they had an Irish trio who played lively tunes. Perhaps that would cheer him up,

Lee thought. He didn't say anything to Grace about the cheating episode. Soon enough there would be time to tell her.

"I think I ought to tell you something about Karen," Beth began as they were eating their Irish stew and drinking Guinness.

"What's that, Mother?" Grace asked.

"She isn't coming home at night lately. She's staying over with that headmaster from St. Bonnie's, and I just don't think that is proper." Beth looked at Grace and then at Lee, finally at Sean.

Sean smiled broadly. "That suits me just fine," he said, " Because that means I can stay with your mother and that's very nice."

"Mother, you can hardly criticize Karen for going over and sleeping with Ted Walker when you are entertaining Sean O'Toole in your own bedroom."

Lee thought Grace was trying to sound like the modern woman who believes in freedom of everything for her gender.

"But we're going to get married," Sean interrupted. "I'm taking this beauty to Ireland as soon as me ship comes in."

Are you getting married on the pier? Lee thought, but did not say aloud.

"In fact," Sean continued. "Paddy is selling tickets here for the Irish Sweep Stakes and I intend to buy the winning number. Could you maybe let me have ten dollars to get one tonight?"

Lee cut his eyes at Grace but he gave Sean a ten dollar bill and the little man went to the bar and came back with a stub for his Irish sweepstakes ticket.

"The luck of the Irish, my sweet," He said and waved the ticket under Beth's nose. "This is going to make you Mrs. Sean O'Toole and take the both of us to the Emerald Isle. You'll see."

They finished their meal and went their separate ways. Later that night, Lee related the morning events and the cheating and told Grace of his quarrel with Ted.

"I can't stay at St. Bonnie's any longer," Lee said. "Not only am I unhappy there and doing a job I don't like; now I am having to watch a headmaster destroy the integrity of the school. I hope that job at the newspaper comes through soon."

Graduation soon followed and Ted Walker got up before the class of graduating seniors and talked about "Truth, Honor, and the Will to Work". Lee felt like he might throw up. But the seniors tossed their mortar boards into the air and rushed off into the night for a round of parties. Lee just hoped none of them would be killed in drunken driving accidents. That there would be alcohol flowing he had no doubt.

Neither Grace nor Lee was prepared for the note they found in their apartment when they finally got home. It read.

My dear children,

Just like he said, Sean won the Irish sweep stakes. Not the biggest prize but enough for us to carry out our plans. We are leaving for Atlanta and will get married there. Then we fly to Shannon, Ireland where we will stay till the money runs out I guess. I am happier than I have ever been in my life so I hope you will agree that this is the best thing for us to do. I don't want to be a burden on you two and that is what I felt like until Sean O'Toole came into my life. Thank you for all you have done for me—coming to get me out of that horrible prison, giving me a place to live and being good to me. I feel that Sean is heaven sent after the trials I have had with men in the past. He will be good for me and I know I will love Ireland. I give you my blessings and I hope we have yours.

With love to you both always,
Mother

"I can't believe it," Grace said. She put the letter on the kitchen table. "Want a glass of milk?" she asked. "I am not sure I want wine until I digest what this note says and means."

"I think it means they are gone," Lee said. He took Grace's hand. "It's the best thing in the world that could have happened, can't you see that?"

"You're right of course," Grace poured two glasses of milk without waiting for Lee to say he wanted some. "You've been so good during this whole thing, Lee. I appreciate you and love you more than I thought possible. You are truly a good man, too good for me."

"But not good enough for St. Bonnie's," Lee said. "Wonder if Karen will move in with Ted this summer. You can bet she is not going to stay in the apartment alone."

"She's a big girl," Grace said, "And it's time she looked out for herself. Let's go to bed. I have to be up at school early in the morning to close out some matters."

Grace went right to sleep, but Lee tossed and turned for a long time wondering how things would work out for Grace and him. He wished he had bought a ticket in the Irish sweepstakes as well. It was his ten dollars that Sean had used to buy the ticket. No point worrying about that. Sean and Beth were gone, and he thought that his money had been well spent.

Lee rode with Grace to school the following morning. He wanted to be sure his office was cleared out.

Most of the faculty was still around closing out classrooms and storing material until the fall term.

There was bedlam in the teachers' lounge when Lee and Grace entered. The buzz of conversation stopped immediately. Grace went over and poured herself a cup of coffee. Lee stood in the doorway and watched the scene before him.

"OK", Grace said. "What's going on/? Why the silent treatment?"

More silence. Finally the same math teacher that Lee had proctored for spoke up. "They're gone." she said.

"Who's gone?" Grace asked.

"Karen and Ted Walker," the teacher said.

"Gone where for heaven's sake?"Grace looked around the room.

"It seems," one of the male teachers said, "That the headmaster and the public relations director have eloped and gone to Memphis where they will be associated with River View School in that city.'

"How do you know that's true?" Grace asked. She appeared stunned.

"Ted called the chairman of the board last night and

told him they were leaving early this morning. That man's wife called one of the faculty. The news then spread like wild fire."

"It still might be just a rumor,"Grace said slowly.

"No, it's true," said a voice coming into the room. The chairman of the board walked in. "I'm glad you all are assembled here for I have an announcement to make. It is true that Headmaster Walker has left and that Karen Garland has gone with him. It is my understanding that they are to be married and he associated with a school in Memphis. We wish them well. But I have more news, better news I hope. I want to announce that the board has just met in an early morning emergency meeting, and we have elected Grace Garland Castleberry as our interim headmaster, er, headmistress. Congratulations, Grace."

A roar of approval went up from the room and clapping began.

"I don't know what to say," Grace blushed.

Lee came to her side. "Better be quiet then," he whispered. "Intelligent, uppity women win again."

The receptionist came in. "There's a phone call for you, Lee," she said. "You can take it in the office if you like."

Lee entered the office and picked up the phone.

"Lee, it's Bob Reading. The senior editor here wants to talk to you."

"Lee," the editor began. "We are prepared to offer you the position of feature editor, that is if you are still interested."

"You bet I'm still interested," Lee almost shouted.

"Well come on down and we'll get all the paper work done. By the way, your first assignment will be to do a feature article on St. Bonaventure School. Think you can handle that"?

Lee smiled. "I can do that," he said.

ACKNOWLEDGMENTS

This book was originally written in 2004 as part of the National Novel Writing Month, which is an annual challenge to writers to complete a 50,000 word novel during the month of November.

There is no financial reward, no promise of publication, no trophy other than a certificate issued upon verification of the correct number of words.

Upon completion of the contest, I put the file away and did not look at it again until the spring of 2006 when I got it out and printed it. I then decided there was a story here and proceeded to edit it and ready it for publication.

This is the result of that experience, and therefore I am most grateful to National Novel Writing Month for the motivation.

I would also like to thank my author friend, Bay Lott, for helpful suggestions and proofreading, and my reading friend, Margaret Odom, for her assistance. And as always, thanks to Carolyn Mayson Miller for all her creative artistry and graphic expertise.

And, I challenge you to enter the National Novel Writing Month and find out for yourself how much fun and how rewarding this writing assignment can be.

ABOUT THE AUTHOR

Margaret Boland Ellis was born in Meridian, Mississippi, and attended Meridian High School, Mississippi State College for Women, now Mississippi University for Women, and received her degree in English and Journalism from the University of Mississippi.

She spent a number of years working for Eastern Air Lines and in newspaper and public relations work. She has taught journalism and creative writing at the high school and college level.

She was the first woman Little League manager in the state of Alabama, and one of the first soccer coaches in Mobile. She has also coached basketball, volleyball, tennis, track and field, and softball.

When actively playing tennis, she was ranked in the Southern Lawn Tennis Association and the state of Alabama.

Mother of three grown children and five grandchildren, she now resides on the Gulf Coast where she continues writing and directing her own publishing firm, Magnolia Mansions Press.

Other Books

By

Margaret Boland Ellis

Be Good Sweet Maid
Golden Memories of Navy Blue

The Shamrock Diary
Writing as Megan O'Meara

A Wind Called Frederic

A Brief Garland

The Irish Pioneer

Manifold Sins

www.ingramcontent.com/pod-product-compliance
Lightning Source LLC
Chambersburg PA
CBHW071350170626
46811CB00003B/1069

* 9 7 8 0 9 7 5 9 3 9 7 4 1 *